THEODORA HENDRIX
and the MONSTROUS LEAGUE of MONSTERS

THEODORA HENDRIX
and the MONSTROUS LEAGUE of
MONSTERS

JORDAN KOPY

illustrated by Chris Jevons

WALKER
BOOKS

First published 2020 by Walker Books Ltd
87 Vauxhall Walk, London SE11 5HJ

2 4 6 8 10 9 7 5 3 1

Text © 2020 Amanda Kopy Jordan
Illustrations © 2020 Chris Jevons

The right of Jordan Kopy and Chris Jevons
to be identified as author and illustrator respectively
of this work has been asserted by them in accordance
with the Copyright, Designs and Patents Act 1988

This book has been typeset in Berkeley Oldstyle Book

Printed and bound by CPI Group (UK) Ltd, Croydon CR0 4YY

British Library Cataloguing in Publication Data:
a catalogue record for this book is available from the British Library

ISBN 978-1-4063-9261-6

www.walker.co.uk

MIX
Paper from
responsible sources
FSC® C020471

The Most Secret Secret

I'm going to tell you a secret. And not just any old secret. I'm going to tell you a big – no, huge – no, *mega* – secret. The biggest secret there ever was.

But perhaps I shouldn't. Your parents will be furious, and I have quite enough to be getting on with already; I certainly don't need an angry horde of parents on my doorstep.

You see, your parents spend a lot of time telling you things that aren't true (not that they're liars – I would never call your parents liars…).

What sort of lies?

Well, I bet they've warned you against eating ice cream for breakfast. They have undoubtedly said it can make you sick. This is a lie! A fallacy! A gross miscarriage of justice! Ice cream for breakfast is

perfectly safe
and delicious
and I encourage
you to sneak
some from the
freezer when your
dad or babysitter or
grandmother who smells like
mothballs isn't looking. Trust me, *they're* eating it
when *you're* not looking.

But there are bigger lies they tell you too.

Like at bedtime, after they've read you a story
and tucked you in and brought you seventy-four
glasses of water, they probably do one more thing:
check under your bed for monsters. Maybe they
look in your wardrobe, too. They probably say
there's nothing there. They might even say monsters
don't exist. This is also a lie. A fallacy. A gross –
maybe even fatal – miscarriage of justice.

Because, of course, they do exist. Monsters, that is.

That howling you hear at night? It's not the wind,
but a werewolf moaning at the moon. That tapping

at your window? It's not a branch, but a vampire inviting himself in for a snack of your blood. That creaking in the hallway? It's not just "the house settling", but a hag creeping towards your bedroom – they keep children as pets, you know.

Don't believe it? I didn't either. But after you've seen a mummy and been chased by ogres and walked right through a ghost – well, you'd believe it too. And, *no*, I can't tell you who I am or why I've met so many monsters … not yet. For now, let's just say I'm an interested party.

What's that? You *still* don't believe it? That's a shame. You're wrong, you know. The fact of the matter is, monsters live among us.

Just ask Theodora Hendrix.

The Monstrous League of Monsters, 13 Battington Lane, Appleton Village, Pumpkinshire, England, Europe, Earth

It was just shy of midnight on Halloween. Children were running amok in the village of Appleton, dressed as ghosts or skeletons or witches or – you get the idea. The children scurried from house to house, happily trick-or-treating among the pumpkins. Their parents followed willingly enough. (Are you missing a Snickers? Your dad ate it after you'd gone to bed.) But the one place they refused to go, no matter how much their children pleaded, was the graveyard.

The abandoned cemetery had stood at the edge

of town for as long as anyone could remember. The villagers avoided it at all costs; there were rumours of strange happenings there, especially at night.

"You are never to step foot inside the graveyard," the parents of Appleton told their children.

Though it pains me to say it, I must admit – this is the one time they are absolutely telling you the truth. *Stay away from graveyards.* Or you just might find yourself face to face with a zombie waking up from a year-long nap.

One such zombie, named Georgie Hendrix, was clawing his way out of the damp earth of a borrowed grave (*his* grave was currently occupied by a particularly vicious hobgoblin with a taste for human flesh). As he wiped the worm-filled dirt from his eyes, Georgie was pleased to find his very best friend, a masked vampire-cat named Bandit, waiting for him.

"Eurgggg," said Georgie, the drooling slash of his mouth twisting into a smile as he roughly patted the cat's head.

"Meow," Bandit replied plaintively. This might have meant, "Why were you asleep for so long?" or, "I've missed you," but I can't be sure – unlike Georgie, I don't speak cat.

Their reunion was suddenly interrupted by a strange, terrible sound. A sound dreaded by people in aeroplanes and restaurants everywhere: the sound of a baby crying.

The friends exchanged looks of alarm.

Georgie rose to his feet on unsteady legs. He stumbled to an unmarked grave where a tiny human swaddled in blankets was wailing like a banshee. Georgie glanced around, peeking behind the tombstones for the baby's minders. Surely they were near by?

But Bandit wasn't so sure. He streaked across the graveyard, darting between the overgrown plots in search of someone – anyone – to whom the tiny squalling human might belong. He returned a few

minutes later, empty-
pawed.

"Eurg?" asked Georgie,
scratching his head.

"Meow," Bandit
replied in dismay.

The baby, it seemed,
was quite abandoned.

Neither Georgie nor
Bandit had the faintest idea
what to do next. They couldn't take
the baby from the graveyard – what if her parents
returned? But they couldn't leave her, either – not
with all those hobgoblins skulking around. As
they mulled it over, a long-fingered, greyish-brown
hand appeared from behind a headstone and began
creeping towards the baby like a spider.

"Meow?" asked Bandit, yellow eyes widening as
the hand inched closer.

"Eurg," Georgie agreed, scooping the baby into
his arms just as the hobgoblin made a grab for her,
hissing like a lobster dropped in a pot of boiling

water. The baby fell silent, teardrops still clinging to her eyelashes.

With a swipe at the hand and a swish of his tail, Bandit led the way out of the cemetery. Georgie lurched after him, hoping they were doing the right thing. They quickened their pace, eager to return home. The other monsters would know what to do with the baby.

Oh yes, there were more of them.

Ten minutes later, Georgie and Bandit were standing before a sprawling mansion owned by a *very* unusual group of individuals who called themselves the Monstrous League of Monsters (we'll call them the MLM for short). Mrs Next Door and Mrs Across the Street were always complaining it was an eyesore, what with the cobwebs and crumbling facade and hulking stone gargoyles, but to Georgie's rotting, gummy eyes it was the most beautiful place in the world.

"Meow?"
Bandit prompted.
He probably
meant, "Are you
going to ring the
doorbell, Georgie?"
or, "Knock on the
door – I can't reach!"

Georgie shook his
head, indicating his
oversized hands full
of the baby.

"Need help, mate?"
called a gargoyle
named Bob from
the turreted roof.

"Eurg."

They heard the scraping
sound of stone against stone
as Bob abandoned his post. He
crossed the roof in two great
leaps, vanishing down a chimney.

"Show-off," muttered Sally, his gargoyle partner-in-crime.

Have you ever dragged your nails down the side of a blackboard? It makes an awful screeching sound (if your teacher is annoying you, I suggest giving it a try). That's the sound the lacquered front door made as it swung open.

A most terrible sight greeted them. Honestly, it's so scary I don't know if I should tell you – I don't need you getting nightmares and crying to your parents, because they might take away this book, and these pages contain very important, life-saving information.

Well, if you insist... Behind the door was a bonadoo named Bon. What's a bonadoo, you ask? A bonadoo is a creature with the body of a hare (similar to a rabbit) and the tawny mane, tufted tail and long teeth of a lion... Did I mention they like to snack on little kids? Well, they do, and as soon as Bon caught sight of the baby he sprang from the floor like a ninja, launching himself right at her. And then he tried to eat her.

Now, I have already told you that the world is full of monsters, but what I *haven't* told you is that there are *good* monsters, like Georgie and Bandit, and *bad* monsters, like Bon. So what was a bad monster doing with the good monsters of the MLM? I'll explain.

The MLM Charter nailed to the wall of the MLM meeting room lists three rules:

1. *Keep monsters hidden from humans*
2. *Protect humans from bad monsters*
3. *Help bad monsters become good monsters*

Did you read that last bit carefully? *Help bad monsters become good monsters.* That explains why the bad bonadoo Bon was at the MLM mansion: reform school.

Yes, you read that right.

Reform school is one of the MLM's most important jobs – nearly as important as keeping the existence of monsters hidden from people. Why do monsters stay hidden? Well, just imagine if goo-goo-eyed teenagers could ask witches for love spells, or if politicians could pay werewolves to attack their enemies; it would be chaos – no, bedlam – no, anarchy! Monsters would never know another moment's peace. No, better they stay out of all that human nonsense. Of course, in order to do *that* the good monsters have to keep an eye on the bad monsters … which brings us back to reform school.

Anyway, I bet you're wondering if Bon ate the baby?

Stop biting your nails! I know it's scary but it's a filthy habit and I won't have my agents-in-training behaving in such a way. Oops – strike that last bit. Ignore it. Forget I said it!

Since you're worried – Bon *didn't* eat the baby. It was lucky Georgie was there. He flung his arm over her just as Bon jumped, the bonadoo's teeth sinking into the zombie's shoulder instead of the baby's neck. Georgie didn't mind; his flesh was falling off his bones anyway – what was a little more or less? As for the rancid smell of rubbish and the green blood oozing from the wound … well, that couldn't be helped.

"Bon!" cried a voice so raw the speaker might've eaten nails for dinner. "Stop that! Stop *this instant* or I shall make you eat broccoli every day for a month!"

"Meow," Bandit sighed in relief. Here, I think, we can agree he meant, "Thank goodness Mummy is here!"

I told you about mummies, didn't I?

Rules and Regulations

You're right, I didn't tell you the whole story. Suffice it to say, mummies are some of the most powerful monsters on the planet. (I can't speak of the monsters of Saturn or Mars – that's out of my jurisdiction.) In case you didn't know, mummies are wrapped in whitish cloth bandages from head to toe. And if you ever come across one, and you wish to stay alive, you'd better do exactly what that mummy says.

This mummy was no exception.

Her name? I don't think she has one. The others just call her "Mummy".

"Oh, Bon," Mummy sighed, holding the bonadoo upside down by the ankles. "What are we going to do with you?" Her accent, an elegant lilting Egyptian, always sounded stronger when she was

cross. "And I thought you'd be graduating to **Reform Level Two:** *Bad Monsters Who Want to Be Good*."

Bon snapped his teeth.

"But **Reform Level One:** *Bad Monsters Who Don't Know (or Care) They're Bad,* it is. Helter-Skelter!" Mummy called. "We need your help, please."

The long-time butler appeared immediately, as if he'd been waiting for Mummy's call.

Are you picturing an old man in a starched grey suit, nose sticking up in the air? If so, you're partially correct. Helter-Skelter does wear a suit, but he isn't an old man, and he no longer has a nose; Helter-Skelter is a skeleton.

"You called?" he asked in a deep, mournful voice.

"Yes. Bon attacked Georgie—"

"Eurg," Georgie corrected, jerking his head towards the little human.

"Bon attacked this baby," Mummy amended, "and is thrashing about like an eel. Take him, please. He's already taken a bite out of Georgie and I've just changed my dressings…"

"Of course," Helter-Skelter agreed, taking the

offending creature into his arms.

"Thank you. Georgie, Bandit, you have some explaining to do. To the mausoleum – you can tell the League why you've brought a *human* into the mansion."

She spun on her heel, striding purposefully down the hall. Georgie and Bandit had no choice but to follow: I told you, not even other monsters mess with mummies.

They walked down a long corridor, candelabras drenched in cobwebs dotting the walls. They took a right down another hallway, this one lined with wheezing suits of armour (one of which wriggled

his metal fingers in greeting), and a left into the library, a wondrous room filled with books of every size. At the back stood a once-grand mahogany desk, now chipped and scratched. Sitting atop it was a flickering black-flamed candle, a human skull and a raven. The bird cocked his head to the side as they made their way over.

"Would you mind opening the door, Hamlet?"

No, Mummy wasn't talking to the raven: *his* name was Mousetrap, and he wouldn't have listened to her if she had been. The black-beaked bird took orders from one – er – *thing*, and one thing only: the skull, Hamlet. (*Why* this was so is, alas, a tale for another time.)

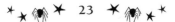

"What's that?" asked Hamlet, bone jaw clattering against the desk.

"Can you open the door, please?" Mummy repeated more loudly.

"Sure thing, ma'am. Apologies, can't hear a thing lately."

"I'll have Helter-Skelter give you a good polish later."

"That'd be lovely, ma'am – ta. Mousetrap?"

At the skull's behest, the raven took flight, soaring towards the tallest bookshelf. He hovered in mid-air over a tattered book, inky wings glinting in the candlelight.

With two sharp pecks of his beak he pushed the book further into the shelf, and then it was moving of its own accord, sinking into the wall as if pulled by an invisible hand. The bookshelf swung forward, revealing a secret passageway. (You didn't think a mansion as haunted as the one at 13 Battington

Lane would fail to have a secret passageway, did you?)

Mummy grabbed a torch from the wall and crossed the threshold, beckoning the others to follow. They did, somewhat reluctantly, the bookshelf slamming behind them. To Georgie and Bandit it was the sound of impending doom.

A sudden chill washed over them. The baby let out a piteous cry. Bandit shivered, from fear as much as cold. But it was only the entrance of Figaro, the operatic ghost.

"Is the MLM still in session?" asked Mummy.

"Yeeeeeeees," sang Figaro.

Reaching a hand right through his stomach, Mummy delivered three sharp raps on a door that blended perfectly into the wall. A narrow strip of wood slid away, revealing two triangle-shaped eyes. One of the pupils (that's the little black centre of your eye) was shaped like a crescent moon, the other a star.

"Password?"

"Coconut-fried cockroaches."

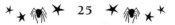

The mismatched eyes vanished. The door creaked open.

"You're just in time for Dracula's update from Headquarters."

"Thanks, Sir Pumpkin-de-Patch the Fourth." (You can just call him Sir Pumpkin-de-Patch. Sir Pumpkin-de-Patch the Fourth is such a mouthful, don't you think?)

They entered the room – an ancient crypt filled with cold, cracked marble. A dozen monsters were scattered about: there was Wilhelmina, a green-skinned witch in a tall, pointed hat; Hilda, a hag, who was staring at the baby with a hungry expression that made Georgie hug the tot closer; Marty, a whiskery werewolf; Grimeny Cricket, a scythe-toting bringer of death in the form of a bug; and Dracula (yes, *the* Dracula), a vampire.

"Ah, Mummy," said Dracula. "Did you take care of the disturbance upstairs?"

"Yes. It was just Bon."

A collective sigh ran

throughout the room; reform school didn't seem to be helping.

"Fine," said Dracula. "If there are no other items to review—"

"I have one," Mummy interrupted. "Bandit has brought Georgie home from his nap."

A smattering of applause filled the chamber. "Well done," said the monsters. "Welcome home, Georgie."

"Yes, well, it seems they haven't returned alone." The applause faltered and then died as Georgie stepped forward. Though the mausoleum was dimly lit, the monsters could see the baby sleeping in the zombie's outstretched arms quite clearly. "They've brought a guest."

"Oh, Georgie," sighed Wilhelmina. "What have you done?"

"What shall we do?" cried Sir Pumpkin-de-Patch.

"Ahem," said Grimeny Cricket, hopping onto the lone workbench that stood among the decaying tombs. "If I may, I suggest we ask Georgie and Bandit *where* they found the human and *why*

they saw fit to bring her here."

"Eurggggg. Eurg-a-eurg," Georgie explained. "Eurg. Euuuuuuurg. Eurg."

"So this baby was all alone? And you're sure her parents weren't somewhere near by?"

Georgie nodded.

"I see," said the bug, adjusting his cloak. "Bandit, do you have anything to add?"

Bandit leapt onto the table. "Me-ow. Me-ooow. Meow."

Now, as I have already told you, I don't speak cat. But I think what Bandit said must have been along the lines of, "It was dark and cold and hobgoblins are the *worst* sort of monsters, who hate eating cake and love eating kids, and one was about to snatch the baby – we had no choice!"

"Thank you, Bandit. That's very helpful."

Bandit nodded imperiously and then began licking his paw.

"Even so," said Wilhelmina with a frown. "You have broken **Rule Number One:** *Keep monsters hidden from humans.*"

"But they have upheld **Rule Number Two:** *Protect humans from bad monsters*," countered Grimeny Cricket.

"What do you think, Mummy?" asked Dracula, dark brows furrowed.

Mummy tucked a loose end of bandage behind her ear, considering. "She's so small, it's unlikely she'll remember any of this," she said slowly. "Perhaps if we just return her…"

"Ah, yes. If we send her back to the humans, then no harm will have been done."

"Eurg?" enquired Georgie, looking concerned.

"Of course. The child will be none the wiser," agreed Dracula. "There will be no punishment, though we will need to report this to Headquarters."

"You did quite well, given the circumstances," chirped Grimeny Cricket. "Then it's settled. We'll return the human to her own kind. But where should we take her?"

"Does she have any identification?" asked Marty the werewolf. "A collar, maybe?"

"She's not a dog, Marty," said Sir Pumpkin-de-Patch scathingly.

"Let's check," Mummy intervened before an argument could begin (Sir Pumpkin-de-Patch had never quite forgiven the werewolf for taking a bite out of his head as a cub; it had taken weeks to grow back). "No," she said, examining the baby, fast asleep in Georgie's arms. "Nothing."

"Then we need to agree where to leave her," decided Wilhelmina.

"A good plan," said Dracula. "Er, any ideas?"

The monsters fell silent, thinking.

"We could take her to Mrs Across the Street," suggested Sir Pumpkin-de-Patch.

"No way, Pumpkinhead. Her garden's too neat," said Marty. "That's no place for a kid – she'll never be allowed to play! How about Mrs Next Door?"

"She cooks cabbage for dinner every night!" cried Sir Pumpkin-de-Patch. "Would *you* want cabbage for dinner every night?"

Marty had to admit he would not.

"Whaaaat about Mr Doooown the Road?" sang Figaro.

"He only watches the news," chided a ghoul

named Gabe, lurking in the corner.

The monsters *tsk*ed and clucked their tongues. They never watched the news if they could help it — it was *so* boring.

"She could stay with me," offered Hilda, licking her lips.

Mummy frowned, not liking the expression on the hag's face any more than Georgie had. She wondered if Hilda needed a refresher, perhaps **Reform Level Seven:** *How to Fight Your Bad Monster Instincts*, or **Reform Level Eleven:** *So You Think You're Going to Relapse.*

"Er, perhaps not," said Dracula. "What about leaving her at a school, or a church?"

"It's the weekend," replied Grimeny Cricket. "There won't be anyone there until Monday. As for a church…"

As you may or may not know, monsters can't step foot in churches. Or synagogues. Or mosques. Or any other holy place. Oh, it's not because the Big Man Upstairs (if you're a believer, you might call him God or Yahweh or Allah or any other number of names) forbids it. It's because of the Monster Secrecy Act. You see, early humans were terrified of monsters, and tried to banish them. They couldn't, of course. Monsters are much too clever and strong. A terrible war was waged. After many losses on both sides, an agreement was reached to keep monsters hidden from humans (with the exception of a few high-ranking government officials) from that point on, and it is this very pact the MLM exists to maintain.

As the monsters pondered what to do, the baby blinked her eyes open. She looked straight at Mummy and smiled a toothless smile. Mummy cooed at her, offering a bandage-wrapped finger. The baby grabbed it. She was surprisingly strong.

"Perhaps," Mummy ventured, "we could keep her here? Just until next week."

"That is most unorthodox," frowned Grimeny Cricket.

But the monsters could think of no other solution, and so it was agreed the baby would remain at the mansion until school started.

"We should give her a name," said Wilhelmina.

A thoughtful expression flickered across Mummy's face. "How about Theodora?" she suggested, squinting at the gurgling baby. "She looks like a Theodora."

"Meow," said Bandit, pausing his bath.

"Quite right," agreed Grimeny Cricket. "Georgie found her, after all."

"That settles it," said Dracula. "Theodora Hendrix, welcome to the MLM."

And that is how Theodora Hendrix came by her name, and how she came to live in a house full of monsters. And honestly, it's not even the strangest thing that's ever happened to her (*that* was meeting the dreadful Ms Frumple – but I'm getting ahead of myself).

Yes, you guessed it. The monsters never returned Theodora to the humans. They meant to (really!) but every time the subject was raised they voted to keep her "just a bit longer".

"She's got a cold," Mummy would say. "We shouldn't send her away sick."

"She's just starting to eat solids," Dracula would argue. "Can't leave the poor dear now."

"She's only just learned to say Sir Pumpkin-de-Patch!"

And so Theodora and the monsters settled into their new lives. Georgie and Bandit did most of the babysitting, Helter-Skelter oversaw feedings, Marty helped with bath time and Mummy did – well, everything else. Despite the extra work, the monsters of 13 Battington Lane were happier than they'd ever been. But

amid their joy a shadow loomed overhead; it was fear, dark and threatening as a storm cloud. Yes, the monsters were frightened. Terrified, even.

"Harbouring a human is punishable by death," Dracula fretted. "If Headquarters ever discovers what we've done…"

"But, Dracula," Mummy replied, changing the baby's nappy with some spare bandages. "You're a vampire – you're already dead!"

"Still," he muttered. "There are other things they can do … things worse than death…"

The monsters fell silent. This, they knew, was true.

"Maybe we should try a bit harder to find her parents," Dracula mused. "They might have left her by mistake, after all. I'll put an ad in the paper and call the hospital and the fire brigade..."

"Whatever you think is best," said Mummy, privately thinking that nobody – not even a human – would leave a baby in a graveyard by mistake.

By the time Theodora had sprouted her first tooth, the question of returning her to any humans was no longer a question at all. By tacit agreement, the monsters added one more rule to the MLM Charter (in invisible ink, of course):

4. Don't let anyone discover Theodora living at the MLM mansion

Of course, someone did.

Little Terrors

We begin the next part of our tale on a Sunday in September, ten years after Georgie and Bandit rescued baby Theodora. The cloudless blue sky promised a perfect day for exploring, or maybe a game of fetch with the werewolf cubs.

A ray of sunlight shimmered through the bat-embroidered curtains at Theodora's bedroom window, warming her skin. She opened her grass-green eyes, blinking to adjust to the brightness of morning. The roman numerals on the old-fashioned alarm clock next to her bed read eight a.m. She wiped the sleep from her eyes, turning her head towards the window. It was then that she saw it.

There – mere centimetres from the ends of her curly red locks – was a great hairy spider. No, it was much larger than a normal spider. It was a tarantula.

Theodora didn't even scream.

Now, I don't know about you, but if I ever found myself face to face with a spider the size of a dinner plate, I would definitely scream. I would jump out of bed, run down the stairs and make scrambled eggs (I never said it would make sense, I just said it's what I would do).

Theodora, however, was not afraid of spiders – not even great hairy ones – and didn't much like scrambled eggs. Instead, she said, "Morning, Sherman."

"Morning, Theodora," replied Sherman the tarantula. "Did you sleep well?"

"Y-y-yes," she yawned.

"Good. Breakfast time, I think. Shall we get dressed?"

Theodora's stomach rumbled in answer. She crossed the carpeted floor to the door, which Mummy always left slightly ajar, and padded barefoot down the hall to the bathroom. She washed her face, brushed her teeth and considered running a comb through her hair, but decided this was overkill for the weekend.

She returned to find Sherman already dressed. He wore a top hat set at a jaunty angle on his head and a monocle upon each of his eight milky eyes (tarantulas have terrible eyesight).

Theodora threw on her favourite tartan skirt and scuffed red trainers. Sherman scuttled up her arm, settling on her shoulder.

"Shall we?" he asked.

"The cards," Theodora reminded him.

"Ah, yes."

Every morning before breakfast, Theodora consulted her torat cards, a gift from Georgie. Now, some of you may have heard of *tarot* cards, which are used by creepy, crystal-laden fortune tellers to understand the past, assess the present and predict the future. *Torat* cards work in a similar way, except for a couple of big differences.

The first is that torat cards don't work for grown-ups; if your nosy mum or even nosier teacher tried to read them, they wouldn't be able to – they'd just see a regular deck of playing cards. The second is that torat cards are created by the elusive rata-tat-tats *especially* for the kid who'll be reading them. (If you've ever met a fashionable lady wearing oversized sunglasses, too many necklaces and bright red lipstick, congratulations, you may have actually seen one!)

Still confused? Don't worry, Theodora is going to demonstrate how it works.

Theodora shuffled the hand-painted cards, cutting the deck in half once they were sufficiently mixed, and randomly selected three cards, laying them side-by-side on her unmade bed.

The first card, which represented Theodora's past, featured a golden-haired woman.

"*The Lady*," Sherman observed. "Mystery. Secrets. The Unknown."

"As usual," said Theodora; Dracula's search for her human family had never uncovered anything. To that day, no one knew who Theodora's birth parents were, why they had left her in the graveyard or what had become of them since.

The second card represented her present.

"*The Castle*," said Sherman, squinting at the turreted structure stretching into a sky swirling with stars. "Disruption. Conflict. Change."

"Hmm. That's new."

The third card, representing Theodora's future, offered a ghoulish Grim Reaper in a billowing cape.

"*Death*," said Sherman, his voice tight with worry. "Unexpected. The End."

"Or the Beginning," she countered, unconcerned. "Remember what Georgie said when he was teaching us how to read the cards? Death can be an ending *or* a beginning."

As it turns out, they were both right. Something was about to begin. And something – or some*one* – was about to end. But we'll get to that later.

Theodora shoved the cards into her pocket. She strolled down the hall, Sherman swaying on her shoulder, and paused at the top of a marvellous staircase with hundreds of pairs of human eyes inlaid in the ivory, winking up at them. The steps themselves were *moving* (one of the mansion's many excellent defences), though the motion ceased as Theodora skipped down their length.

"Morning, Theodora, Sherman," Mummy greeted them as they entered the kitchen. A cauldron full of thick, purple liquid bubbled over a stone hearth in one corner, a great cast-iron stove dominated the other and a stainless steel fridge glinted between them.

"Morning," they replied, settling on a three-legged stool beside the kitchen counter.

"What would you like for breakfast? Fried eggs? Bacon? Boiled beetles?"

"Do we have any leftover pizza?"

"Yes," said Mummy. "But I'm not so sure about pizza for breakfast. How about we save that for lunch, and for now I'll make you some buttered toast?"

"Fine," Theodora sighed. She would never understand the aversion to pizza for breakfast. As far as she was concerned, pizza should be served at every meal (as long as it wasn't topped with pineapple, which is *disgusting* when paired with tomato sauce and cheese).

"May I have my toast with strawberry jam?" Sherman asked hopefully.

"Yes, you may."

"Goody," said Sherman, rubbing his pincers together in anticipation.

"Now remember," said Mummy a few minutes later, tipping some buttered and jammed toast onto their plates. "There's a very important MLM meeting tonight."

"We know," Theodora and Sherman chorused.

"We are not to be interrupted."

"We kno-ow," they repeated. They were given the same speech every week.

"I'll need you to watch the cubs and keep them away from the mausoleum. Last time they got in halfway through Gabe's update on the new Ghoul Management Strategy – not that we didn't need the distraction, it was dreadful – and nearly crushed Grimeny Cricket. This is a *very* important job; I need you to take it seriously."

"Mummy, we know. *Seriously*," Theodora replied, sliding off her stool.

"And, Theodora," Mummy said, a stern look upon her face, "no *funny* business today: if I hear that you've snuck into the Ancient-Curse-Breaking Room – *again* – without permission, or that you've taken any of Helter-Skelter's homemade party mix…"

"I won't," Theodora promised, scooping Sherman into her palm and hurrying from the room before Mummy could lecture them some more. "Geeze," she said, slowing once they were sufficiently far away from the kitchen. "You release one teeny, *tiny* curse into the mansion and you're branded a criminal for life!"

"Theodora," said Sherman, "that curse made anyone who came into contact with it sprout tentacles all over their body! I must say, it was most uncomfortable."

"Still," she muttered. "Wilhelmina got rid of them in the end."

That morning Theodora and Sherman found plenty to keep themselves busy. That was the great thing about living in a haunted mansion – there was always something interesting going on.

They spent an hour catching vampire-mice (slippery little fellows) with Bandit.

They strummed their guitars with Georgie. (Theodora could play two full songs – "Hot Cross Bats" and "Mary Had a Little Toad".)

They even stewed newts (just the tails – and don't worry, they grow back) with Wilhelmina.

"What shall we do now?" asked Sherman as they left the library, having just restacked the books. (As neither Hamlet nor Mousetrap had hands, they welcomed Theodora's assistance, even if it wasn't offered for purely unselfish reasons. She'd come across some real gems that way – books Mummy would've *never* allowed her to read because they were "too mature", including *Bad Banshees and the Men Who Love Them* and *The Hound of Galway*.

"We haven't seen Figaro for a while," Theodora replied, entering the Hall of Reflection. It was made entirely of mirrors, giving the strange impression there were dozens of Theodoras and Shermans (several of whom waved as they passed). At one end, a door opened into a plain little room that housed the Wall of Shame, featuring the portraits of two disgraced former MLM members

– a scowling troll and a haughty-looking hag with a walking stick – positioned beneath three heads.

Yes, heads.

The one on the left was that of a long-eared, ruby-eyed rabbit. The one on the right was a clever-looking fox. The head between them was a deer with gilded antlers.

"Going to the music chamber?" asked the fox, a grin sliding onto his face.

"Yes, we thought we'd visit Figaro."

"Lovely," said the rabbit, and the deer nodded in agreement. "Go on."

Theodora reached towards the silk wall, pressing against a tiny tear in the fabric. The wall shivered. A door appeared where moments before none had stood. She grabbed hold of the tarnished doorknob, twisting it to reveal a winding flight of stairs. Up they climbed, and a few minutes later found themselves in a beautiful room with stained-glass windows and musical instruments of every kind: the usual, such as pianos, and the *un*usual, such as a xylophone made of crocodile teeth. And there, dressed in his finest tuxedo, was Figaro.

"Theodoooora, Shermaaaan," he sang. "What a pleasant surpriiiiise. I was just abooout to praccctise my scaaaales. Would you caaaare to assiiiiist?"

"Sure," they replied. It was an easy job; all they had to do was clap politely as Figaro warbled over the notes, his voice rising and falling gloriously. After some time they headed back downstairs (there was only so much opera, beautifully as it was performed, that one girl and one tarantula could take). Before they knew it, the cuckoo clock in the hallway was clucking. "Nine o'clock, nine o'clock!" the skeletal frame of the bird shouted into the dark.

"Thanks for watching the cubs," said Marty, depositing six little werewolves into Theodora's room.

"No problem," she replied, hoping they'd be better behaved than last time, when they'd chewed through her favourite pair of shoes and eaten two hair ties.

They weren't.

They climbed the furniture, tore the curtains, scared Pimms the Poltergeist to death – or at least they would have, if Pimms could have died *again*. They even chased after Sherman, snapping their jaws and swiping their claws until Theodora put them all in time out.

"I'm too old for this," Sherman moaned, gratefully accepting the spotted handkerchief Theodora handed him. "My poor nerves can't take it. And I've lost a monocle…"

"We'll tell Mummy we need more help next time," Theodora agreed, plucking the missing eyepiece from the snout of a cub and passing it to Sherman. "Maybe we can ask Helter-Skelter…"

"Thanks," said Sherman, pressing the handkerchief to his brow. "And Theodora?"

"Yes?"

"One of the cubs has escaped," he said, pointing a long, hairy leg at the door.

"What?" she yelped, following the direction of Sherman's limb. "Oh, no."

"You get him; I'll watch the others," Sherman called as she raced from the room.

Theodora chased the errant cub (she was nearly certain it was Sylvester – it was *always* Sylvester) down the corridor and into the library. She burst into the room just in time to see his little tufted tail vanish into the secret passageway. He was headed straight for the mausoleum.

Of course he was.

"We tried to stop him," cried Hamlet the skull, "but he's too quick!"

"Don't worry," she said, grabbing a torch off the wall. "I'll catch him!"

Theodora ran as fast as she could down the dark passageway, footsteps echoing against the stone floor. She could hear the cub panting and snarling some metres ahead. "Gotcha," she gasped, grabbing him round the middle and bundling him into her arms like a rugby ball.

The cub giggled.

"Bad werewolf!" she cried.

Sylvester began licking her face, not the least bit chastened.

"You must learn to follow instructions," Theodora said in the stern voice Mummy used when she was frustrated with her for not eating all her frog legs or for forgetting to do her homework. "Otherwise…"

But something caught Theodora's eye, distracting her from finishing her sentence.

It would have distracted you, too.

The Letter

Someone had left the mausoleum door ajar. *That won't do*, thought Theodora. The meetings were meant to be private, and who knew what sorts of creatures (other than naughty werewolf cubs) were crawling around the passageways?

"Shh," she ordered Sylvester, pressing a finger to her lips. She crept forward with the cub still in her arms, intending to close the door without attracting the monsters' attention, but then heard something that gave her pause:

"We received a suspicious letter two days ago," said Owen, a ghostly owl who'd been heading up the MLM Post Office for the past three years. "No postmark. No address."

"What did it say?" asked Sir Pumpkin-de-Patch.

"It said, *I know what you did, and I'm going to tell.*
That's all."

The monsters pondered this for several moments.

"But what could it mean?" Wilhelmina wondered.

"I'm not sure. But there was a sticky substance
coating the envelope," replied the owl, clamping
the letter in his beak so the monsters could see. He
dropped it back on the table, clicking in distaste.
"We think it's earwax."

"Erghhhh," the monsters groaned.

"Disgusting," grunted Marty.

"Excellent healing properties, though," Wilhelmina allowed, thinking she might use some in her next potion.

"Well, it's an *inordinate* amount of earwax," Owen continued. "Which can only mean…"

"Trolls," Grimeny Cricket finished. "Only trolls' ears drip with so much wax."

"But Headquarters has banned the European Troll Cluster from all MLM-related activities for eighteen months," said Dracula. "And that includes contacting all MLM agencies."

"True," Mummy agreed. "But when have trolls ever followed the rules?"

"We're focusing on the wrong thing, I'm afraid," said Grimeny Cricket, adjusting his cloak. "We should be dissecting what the letter means, not who sent it."

"But if we know *who* sent it we might be able to figure out *why* they sent it," argued Sir Pumpkin-de-Patch.

"Pumpkinhead's got a point," said Marty, scratching his chin with a claw.

The meeting dissolved into chaos, the monsters talking loudly over one another as they quarrelled over what the letter might mean and who might have sent it.

Unnoticed, Theodora closed the door. She edged back down the corridor, still cradling an unusually still Sylvester. Neither made a peep as she climbed back into the library: Theodora was thinking about what she'd overheard and Sylvester was tired from his illicit adventure.

As for me, I have some idea what the letter was about. I've been working on a theory for some time … but perhaps we need to gather more evidence. There's a method to these things, you know.

The shrill screech of the alarm clock woke Theodora early on Monday morning.

"Hit the snooze button," Sherman murmured,

pulling his nightcap lower over his eyes.

"Can't," Theodora replied, jumping out of bed. "Today's the first day of the new term – don't want to be late."

Sherman groaned and went back to sleep. Theodora didn't mind – Sherman wasn't one for early mornings. Neither was she, for that matter. But then, Sherman didn't have to go to school.

Theodora had tried bringing him for Show and Tell once. She'd thought her classmates might be interested in meeting a real, live tarantula (of course, she'd had to make Sherman promise not to speak in front of them – Mummy had very strict rules about such things).

Boy, was she wrong!

As soon as she'd opened Sherman's travelling case (a lunchbox with air holes punched into the sides) everyone started screaming, jumping atop their desks or racing for the door – their teacher was even spotted tossing children bodily out of the way in her haste to

escape. Theodora had been given a lecture on what *was* and *wasn't* appropriate for school and sent to Ms Sweet – the head teacher's – office. Ms Sweet was more understanding. She even asked to take a look at Sherman before calling Mummy to pick Theodora up from school.

I know what you're thinking: you're wondering how Mummy could even set foot in a school. After all, wouldn't that break **Rule Number One:** *Keep monsters hidden from humans*?

You're quite right. If Mummy had showed up at school in head-to-toe bandages, why, it would have been ruinous – no, disastrous – no, catastrophic! And if Headquarters had found out that she'd intentionally broken a rule, Mummy would have been severely punished. So how did she manage it?

With a glamour, of course.

Now I'm sure you want to know what a glamour is. I'd better pour myself a cold one (chocolate milk, extra syrup, squiggly straw). A glamour is a spell used by monsters to make themselves appear "normal" to humans. Wilhelmina could brew all sorts

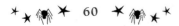

of witchy glamour potions. She had
one that made Dracula look like a
businessman. One that transformed
Marty into a car salesman. She
could even prepare one that made
Helter-Skelter look like a real butler,
nose and all. The one she brewed
for Mummy made her look like your
average school mum.

Anyway, after a quick breakfast
of porridge with sugar (lots of sugar)
Theodora slung her rucksack over her shoulder,
kissed Mummy goodbye and headed to school.

"Hi, Bandit," she said, meeting him at the
wrought iron gates lining the MLM property.

"Meow," Bandit chirruped, winding himself
between her ankles in greeting.

He led the way down Battington Lane, tail high
in the air. Bandit would take her as far as Orchard
Street. From the corner, he'd watch as Theodora met
the lollipop woman, crossed the street and entered
Appleton Primary School. Then he'd go back to

the mansion and ask Georgie to play his favourite song, "Wonder-caterwaul", to lull him into a nap. At three-thirty sharp, Bandit would return to the corner of Orchard Street and bring Theodora home.

If only Theodora had known the terrible thing waiting for her at school today. She would have stayed at home, pretending to be sick or played truant (that means skip school and, *no, you're not allowed to do that!*). But, alas, Theodora *didn't* know what awaited her, and unsuspectingly made her way into the red brick building.

A few minutes later she was settling at her desk, which had a neat little drawer for her books and a hook for her bag. A low hum of chatter filled the room, her classmates comparing notes on the summer holidays and wondering what their new teacher would be like. No one asked Theodora about her holidays, but then she hadn't expected them to; Theodora didn't have many friends – at least, she didn't have many *human* friends. In fact, she didn't have any at all. Not that she minded (or so she told herself).

"Welcome to Year Five," said a heavy-jawed woman, stepping to the front of the class. "My name is Mrs Dullson, and I'll be your teacher."

"Good morning, Mrs Dullson," the class chanted.

"You may have noticed your class of twenty-five has grown to twenty-six," she continued, gesturing to a desk in the middle row. "Class, please welcome Dexter Adebola."

"Looks at those glasses!" snickered Billy Ellis, a boy with a habit of picking his nose when he thought no one was looking. "Hello, Four-Eyes!"

The whole class laughed, except for Theodora. She didn't think it was very funny – or very nice – to make fun of someone's appearance.

"That's enough, Billy," said Mrs Dullson, pursing her lips as if she'd eaten something sour. "Dexter,

why don't you stand and introduce yourself to the class?"

The metal chair scraped against the floor as Dexter rose to his feet. He was rather small, and wore a yellow waistcoat and khaki trousers. Theodora had the feeling he would rather be anywhere else, for his voice shook as he said, "I'm D-Dexter. My family just moved h-here from America."

"Thank you, Dexter," said Mrs Dullson. "You may sit down. Now class – yes, Dexter?"

"M-my mom said I was s-supposed to take this note to the nurse. It's my l-list of allergies," he stammered, pushing his thick, black-framed glasses higher on his nose.

"Very well. Who would like to take Dexter to Nurse Josephine?"

The class eyed each other, wondering who would volunteer. Theodora stuck her hand into the air.

"Thank you, Theodora," said Mrs Dullson. "Do come right back."

As they exited the room, Billy whispered, "See you later, *Four-Eyes!*"

"Ignore him," Theodora sighed, pulling the door closed behind them. "I do."

"S-sorry you got s-stuck taking me," sniffed Dexter.

"Don't be silly," said Theodora, leading him down the sterile hallway. "What are you allergic to, anyway?"

"Everything," Dexter said sadly. "Dogs, cats, dust, p-peanuts..."

"Good thing you're letting the nurse know. People bring peanut butter sandwiches for lunch sometimes."

"I was afraid of that. Now e-everyone will h-hate me more than they already do!"

"I don't hate you," said Theodora. "And besides, who cares what they think?"

Before Dexter could marvel at the idea of not caring about what others thought, Theodora saw something that made her spine tingle.

Earwax. Lots of earwax.

The Most Villainous Villain

Are you thinking what I'm thinking? Earwax was all over the mysterious letter sent to the MLM Post Office, and now it was appearing at Appleton Primary School? I don't think it can be just a coincidence. Neither did Theodora.

"Hmm," she said, taking a step closer to examine it. Two trails of the thick yellowish substance, positioned several metres apart, had congealed on the floor. Remembering what Owen had said about the earwax most likely coming from trolls, Theodora wondered if the two distinct tracks meant there was more than one. Or maybe it had leaked out of both ears of a single troll?

"W-what's that?" asked Dexter.

"Earwax, I think," Theodora replied, kneeling

down for a better look.

"Earwax? Where did it c-come from?"

"A troll, probably," she muttered to herself.

"What?" he yelped.

"Never mind," said Theodora, standing. "Listen, Dexter, I've got to see where this goes. It could be important. Do you think you can go to the nurse by yourself? It's not far."

Dexter's eyes widened in alarm, his eyebrows disappearing beneath his hair.

"Fine," she sighed. "We'll follow the trail, then go to the nurse together."

"B-but won't we get in t-trouble?" worried Dexter, hurrying to catch up with Theodora, who was already halfway down the corridor.

"Only if we get caught."

They followed the uneven trail, careful to avoid stepping in it, to a pair of metal doors.

"Looks like it leads outside," said Theodora.

"I g-guess that's it, then," said Dexter, visibly relieved.

"What are you talking about?" Theodora asked,

pushing the heavy doors open.

"B-but…"

"You can stay here if you like," she said, stepping into the pale September sunshine.

Dexter considered his options. He definitely didn't want to break a rule – and he was almost certain going outside without permission was breaking a rule – but he was also afraid to wait by himself. What if one of the Year Six students passed by? Or, worse, a teacher?

"Wait for me!" he called, hurrying after her. Seconds later, poor Dexter was rewarded for his daring by running headlong into Mr Jackson, the caretaker.

"And just where do you think you're goin'?"

"I-I-I…"

"We were just going for a tour of the playing field," said Theodora quickly. "Dexter is new. Mrs Dullson asked me to show him around."

"Students aren't allowed out of doors without a teacher," admonished the caretaker.

"Sorry, Mr Jackson. I forgot."

"I'll have to take you to the head teacher's office."

Theodora sighed. Dexter went green around the edges.

"Mr Jackson?" Theodora asked tentatively as they walked. "Can I ask you a question?"

He grunted non-committally.

"Where did that trail of … stuff … lead? It looked like it suddenly stopped just outside the doors."

"Been cleanin' it up all mornin'," he groused. "Went all over, it did."

"Where?" Theodora pressed.

But they were already outside Ms Sweet's office. Mr Jackson knocked on the warped glass windowpane fitted into the door.

"Come in."

Theodora straightened her hair ribbon. "Come on, Dexter. Let's get this over with," she said, pushing her way into the office.

Have you ever met someone you disliked on sight? I have. So has Theodora – or at least she will, as she's about to meet our villain (or, rather, *one* of them), the terrible Ms Frumple. And trust me, Ms Frumple wasn't your run-of-the-mill villain. She's the worst villain there ever was.

I can see you're sceptical. I know what you're thinking: it's all over your face (you should *never* play poker). You're thinking there are a great many villains sprinkled throughout books, films, plays and television shows – not to mention in real life – who are absolutely atrocious. So what could possibly make Ms Frumple worse than any of *them*?

I'll explain.

By definition, villains aren't very nice people. But at least they have goals. Off the top of my head, I can think of the goals of some of the most hated villains of all time: take over the wizarding world, curse the princess into an everlasting sleep, make a coat out of puppies. Ms Frumple, on the other hand, had none. And that's a sign of true evil: evil for evil's sake. Well, maybe that's overstating things a bit... Ms Frumple *did* have one goal, but it's too great – too terrible – to name.

Fine, have it your way. Just don't say I didn't warn you.

It was Ms Frumple's greatest ambition to rid the world, or at least Appleton Primary, of anyone who was "different" from her. As far as Ms Frumple was concerned, if you didn't look like her or talk like her and preferred your steak cooked any way other than medium rare (fine, I'll give her that one), well, she simply had no use for you, and she'd do everything in her considerable power to get rid of you. Now in my book (including this one), hating someone just because they're different from you … well, that's truly evil.

I'm sure you've realized by now that Theodora isn't exactly like other people. I suppose being raised by monsters has something to do with it. Ms Frumple scented it – this *differentness*. And she was determined to put a stop to it.

Theodora entered the office without waiting for permission – Ms Sweet wouldn't have minded. But as you have already guessed, it was not Ms Sweet who awaited her.

"Who are you?" Theodora asked rather rudely, still gripping the doorknob, Dexter hovering behind her.

The woman sitting behind the desk must have thought it rude too, for she said, "I'm Ms Frumple, the new head teacher, and I expect to be addressed as 'ma'am'. Come in, both of you."

Theodora didn't move. "What happened to Ms Sweet … ma'am?"

"Not that it's any of your business," sniffed Ms Frumple, "but she's retired. *You* are?"

RULES OF CONDUCT

1. No smiling
2. No laughing
3. No talking
4. No sweets
5. No playing
6. No fun
7. No crying

"Theodora Hendrix."

"And the gentleman standing behind you?"

"D-Dexter Adebola," said Dexter in a rather high-pitched voice. "Today's my first d-day."

"I hope you won't make a habit of getting sent to this office, as *some* people seem to do."

"No, ma'am, I w-won't."

"We shall see... Now, what's this about?"

"They was out of bounds," said Mr Jackson, popping his head into the office. "I found them in the playing field." Then he popped his head back out, closing the door behind him with a resounding click.

"Good news travels fast, I guess," said Theodora, flopping into a chair and glancing around the office, which looked remarkably different from how it had when Ms Sweet occupied it. Gone were the framed pieces of student art, the smiling photographs of classes

The Perfect Student

past and, most distressingly, the cookie jar. In their place were oversized posters with titles such as "RULES OF CONDUCT" and the *unsmiling* photographs of Ms Frumple's former students.

HALL MONITORS

Your Headteacher needs
YOU!

"I'll not tolerate that sort of attitude," Ms Frumple frowned as Dexter perched on the edge of his seat like a bird poised for flight. "Do you think breaking school rules is a joke?"

Theodora opened her mouth to say, *So what if I do?* but thought better of it. "No, ma'am," she said, crossing her fingers under the desk. "Sorry."

"I'm afraid sorry's not good enough. I've had a look at your rather large disciplinary file," the head teacher continued, pushing aside the school uniform catalogue she'd been perusing and flipping open a thick manila folder with Theodora's name splashed across it in red. "I see you've

Ms Frumple says:

Don't let your grades slip!

been reprimanded for breaking the dress code, tardiness, missing homework… You also brought a dangerous animal to school, is that correct?"

"Sherman's not dangerous. He wouldn't hurt a fly!"

"Tarantulas eat flies, my dear."

"Not Sherman," Theodora insisted. "He eats toast with jam and mint chocolate chip ice cream and—"

"And now you're telling lies."

"I am not," said Theodora hotly. "Sherman really does eat those things!"

"Detention," hissed Ms Frumple. "Both of you."

"That's not fair!" Theodora cried. "Dexter didn't do anything – he never would've gone outside if it hadn't been for me."

"For a week. Would you like to make it two?"

"P-please," Dexter begged, looking as if he might cry. "Please don't. My parents will be so disappointed…"

"Let it be a lesson to you, Mr Adebola," said Ms Frumple gravely. "You should be more careful in choosing your friends. If I were you," she said, eyes sliding from Dexter's distraught face to Theodora's defiant one, "I'd stay away from *bad influences*."

Theodora's hands balled into fists beneath the desk, but she wisely said nothing.

As if she knew what Theodora was thinking, a reptilian smile spread across Ms Frumple's doughy face. "Let me offer *you* some advice, Ms Hendrix," she said in a soft tone that put Theodora on high alert (when you get into trouble as often as Theodora does, you develop a bit of a radar for these things). "In my school, children who disobey the rules are punished. Children who talk back are punished. Children who are rude are punished." She leaned across the table, so Theodora could see the blood vessels reddening her pale eyes. "Children who do all three will spend a great deal of time in detention. Do you understand?"

"Perfectly," Theodora replied through stiff lips.

Oh, yes, it was hate at first sight.

And Ms Frumple was just getting started.

A Game of Chess

"What's this about detention?" Mummy asked as soon as Theodora walked in the door, rucksack laden with homework. "I got a call from the new head teacher."

Theodora didn't answer right away. If she told Mummy she'd purposely been tracking the earwax, Mummy would want to know why. And then Theodora would have to admit she'd been eavesdropping on the MLM meeting, and Mummy wouldn't be at all pleased. But Theodora also didn't want to lie – especially not to Mummy.

"Well, I was showing my new friend around school," she began carefully.

Mummy brightened. "You've made a friend? A *human* friend?"

"I think so," said Theodora, briefly describing Dexter.

"That's wonderful," said Mummy, clapping her hands together. "Perhaps we can invite Dexter over for tea."

"Er, maybe," said Theodora, recalling the last time she'd had someone over, nearly two years before.

It had been a disaster.

Figaro hadn't realized they had human company, or he would have hidden in the music chamber (glamour potions don't work on ghosts – you need a physical body to transform). He'd floated right through the wall into the room where the children were playing and given Shirley Blair, a pigtailed girl from Theodora's class, the fright of her life. She'd run screaming from the house, and Mummy had received a very angry phone call from Shirley's mother.

Word had got around, and before long none of
the Appleton parents wanted their children going to
that strange Theodora Hendrix's house. Of course,
they didn't really have much choice after the ghost

incident. They couldn't very well have their children running around a haunted mansion when they spent half their lives insisting monsters didn't exist.

"But why did you go outside?" asked Mummy. "Surely you know it's against the rules?"

This was the tricky part. "I saw something odd."

Mummy nodded for her to continue.

"There was a trail of yellowish stuff," she said, haltingly. "It almost looked like earwax…"

Mummy looked up quickly. "Earwax? At school?"

"A lot of it," Theodora confirmed.

"I see," said Mummy, tugging at a loose piece of bandage that had escaped her ponytail. "I need to send a letter to Headquarters, right away. We'll talk more later, OK?"

"Sure," said Theodora. "But I'm starving. Do we have any pizza?"

"In the fridge!" Mummy called over her shoulder as she rushed from the room.

"Hi, Theodora." It was Sherman, helicoptering down from the ceiling on a strand of spider silk.

"Want some pizza?"

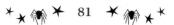

"Yes, please. Can I have strawberry jam on mine?"

"Course," said Theodora, plucking the jar out of the fridge.

"Thanks. How was your first day?"

"Awful." She told Sherman all about the earwax and the horrible Ms Frumple while she waited for the pizza to heat up.

"What a nightmare." Sherman shuddered. "And I agree about the earwax – it can't be just a coincidence. There's something fishy going on."

"I wonder if it has something to do with the torat reading yesterday," Theodora mused, biting into a steaming slice of pizza.

"Perhaps," said Sherman. "What did the cards say this morning?"

"Same thing," she replied through a mouthful of pizza. "Only … never mind."

"Never mind what?"

Theodora hesitated, then pulled the torat pack out of her pocket. She flipped through the deck, searching for one card in particular, *The Castle* (disruption, conflict, change), placing it face up on the worktop. "Does this look any different to you from how it did yesterday?"

Sherman scuttled over, abandoning his jammy pizza. "Hmm. Same stone palace, same starry sky. But, what's that?" He tapped a leg against the upper right-hand corner. "It's hard to see – it's so small – but it looks like some sort of bird... Has that always been there?"

"I don't think so," she replied, wondering again how, and why, the bird had appeared on the card.

"Have the cards ever changed before?" Sherman wanted to know.

"Never."

"Definitely fishy," he murmured. "I'll keep my eyes open..."

"Hi, Theodora," said Dexter the next day, sitting down beside her at registration.

"Hi, Dexter," she replied. "I've been meaning to

tell you, I'm sorry you got detention because of me."

"Oh, I-I didn't. Ms Frumple called my mom and – well, I-I don't have detention any more." He opened his mouth as if to say something else, then closed it. He began chewing on an already ragged fingernail, avoiding Theodora's gaze.

"Are you all right?"

"Y-yes," he replied around his finger. "I-I was just wondering if ... if..."

"If what, Dexter?"

"Would-you-wanna-join-Chess-Club-with-me?"

"No way!" shouted Billy Ellis. "*Four-Eyes* and Theo*bora*?"

Dexter blushed, but Theodora fixed Billy with a steely glare. "Knock it off, Billy."

"Or you'll do what?"

"I'm not sure," said Theodora thoughtfully. "Cast a spell on you, perhaps. I think I'll turn you into a rat. Or maybe a toad."

"There's no such thing as magic, dummy."

"That's what you think," quipped Theodora. "Shirley Blair and I know different…"

Billy paled, quickly turning back to the front of the room, where Mrs Dullson was writing the day's objectives on the whiteboard.

"So immature," Theodora muttered under her breath. Turning back to Dexter, she said, "I would love to join the Chess Club with you. But I can't until next week, after my detentions are over. Ms Frumple has me writing lines," she scowled.

"Great," said Dexter, breaking into a smile. "It meets every Monday after school."

The next few days crawled at a snail's pace, time

passing so slowly Theodora found herself wondering if her watch had stopped working. She couldn't wait for the weekend to end (a totally unprecedented event) and for school to finish that following Monday. It wasn't that she was overly excited about Chess Club – not exactly. It was just such a nice feeling to be included (and by a *human*, no less). Theodora's anticipation, however, was nothing compared to Dexter's.

"You're going to love it," he gushed during lunch. "Chess is so much fun."

His enthusiasm was contagious. Theodora found herself bobbing her head in agreement despite the fact that she'd never played and had no idea whether or not this was actually true.

"Plus my mom always packs extra snacks on Club days," he continued in the same eager tone. "She made popcorn for today! And look," he grinned, pulling out two plastic sandwich bags, miraculously uncrushed despite having sat at the bottom of his dinosaur-patterned lunch box. "She's sent some for you, too!"

"That was nice of her," said Theodora, returning Dexter's grin; she *loved* popcorn (not as much as pizza, but it was close). Although, if she was being honest, she preferred it piping hot, doused in butter and coated in salt – and accompanied by a side serving of chocolate, of course. Unfortunately, when Dexter shared out the popcorn before Chess Club, it became clear that Mrs Adebola was a bit more health conscious. She'd made them plain popcorn with a teeny, tiny bit of butter. No salt. No chocolate. (Parents really know how to take all of the fun out of life, don't they?) But Theodora didn't mind. They were munching away happily when Ms Frumple strode past.

"Having a snack before Chess Club, Mr Adebola?"

"Y-yes, ma'am. My mom s-says I have to maintain my blood sugar levels."

"And Ms Hendrix, what are you doing here?"

"I'm joining Chess Club."

Ms Frumple raised an eyebrow. "You are?"

"Yes," Theodora replied, spraying bits of popcorn all over the head teacher's blazer. "Oops, sorry."

"Delighted to hear it," said Ms Frumple, lip curling in disgust as she brushed away the kernels. "Good to see you branching out into some structured, appropriate activities for a change."

And just like that, Theodora's elation popped like a balloon. *Structured? Appropriate?* The only time those words were used to describe anything she was interested in was – well, never. No, Theodora preferred things that were decidedly *un*structured and *in*appropriate (like stuffing her face full of brownies during PE instead of running laps – *that* was more her style).

"Well, in you go," said Ms Frumple. "We'll be starting shortly."

"*We?*" Theodora sputtered. "You're staying?"

"Of course," she replied, the corners of her mouth turning up as Theodora's fell. "I run Chess Club."

Dexter barrelled into the classroom, an ecstatic

expression upon his face. Theodora followed reluctantly (nothing the odious Ms Frumple was in charge of could be fun, of this she was certain). They settled at a desk, Dexter bouncing in his seat, Theodora slouching in hers and observing the chessboard without much interest.

Have you ever seen a chessboard? I imagine you have. But just in case you haven't, or if you can't remember what it looks like (are you taking your vitamins?), let me fill you in.

A chessboard is similar to a draughts board; both are covered in alternating white and black squares. On one side are sixteen white pieces. On the other side – you guessed it – sixteen black pieces. Each player holds one king, one queen, two rooks, two bishops, two knights and eight pawns. The object of the game is to checkmate (capture) your opponent's king. It is a game of strategy and one at which, I must admit, I excel. (OK, so I'm not *quite* as good as Grimeny Cricket – and, *no*, I'm not going to tell you the sorry tale of how I lost a game of chess to a bug.)

"OK, boys and girls," began Ms Frumple, clapping her hands together to call the group to attention. "Let's begin."

By the time Dexter had finished explaining the rules (in painstaking detail), nearly twenty minutes had elapsed, leaving just enough time for them to play – and for Theodora to lose spectacularly. Twice.

"You've got to focus," Dexter told her, his own brow furrowed in concentration as he slid his bishop across the board, capturing Theodora's remaining rook.

Ms Frumple's
Guide to
Rules and Schoc
Etiquette:

1.
2.
3.
4.
5.
6.
7.

"I am focused!" she replied, eyes roving over the room in search of something more interesting than the heaping pile of pawns Dexter had collected on his side of the board.

She found it.

A crow was perched just outside the dirt-streaked window at the back of the room. It might have been Theodora's imagination (which, it must be said, is a wee bit overactive), but she could have sworn its beady orange eye was looking right at her.

In fact, she was sure of it.

She shifted, craning her neck for a better look. She couldn't quite put her finger on it, but something about the crow made her distinctly uneasy. Perhaps it was the sharpness of its beak (which looked more than capable of pecking out a pair of grass-green eyes), or the unusual stillness of its stance, or the fact that a bird (perhaps a crow?) had appeared in the torat cards just days earlier. Whatever it was, she wished the crow would go away.

"D-do you think w-we have time for another game?" asked Dexter, delivering his second checkmate of the day. "Theodora? H-hello? What're you looking at, anyway?"

"Maybe," said Theodora, glancing at the board without really seeing it. "And nothing."

When she turned back to the window, the crow was gone. Theodora released a breath she hadn't realized she'd been holding.

"Time's up," called Ms Frumple. "Put away your boards and pack up your things."

"That was great," said Dexter, rising to his feet and arranging the straps of his rucksack so the weight was evenly distributed between his narrow shoulders.

"It was," Theodora agreed, slinging her bag over one shoulder and deciding not to mention that she'd found chess a bit boring.

They joined the other students filing out of the classroom and into the hallway, where several parents were milling around.

"Dexter, over here."

"Hi, Mom," he said. "This is Theodora."

"Theodora! Mrs Adebola smiled warmly. She had beautiful white teeth (yes, teeth can be beautiful). "It's so nice to meet you."

"Nice to meet you, too. Thanks for the popcorn," said Theodora, thinking Mummy would be pleased she'd remembered her manners. "I like your scarf," she added, pointing to the brightly coloured cloth wrapped around Mrs Adebola's head.

"Thank you. It's called a gele," Dexter's mum explained. "My sister sent it from Nigeria."

"Are you Nigerian, then?"

"Yes. Adebola is a West African name."

"Cool," said Theodora. "Mine is Zombian."

If either Mrs Adebola or Dexter found this to be strange, they were too polite to say.

"Thanks for inviting me along, Dexter. I had a really good time," Theodora said.

"No prob. Hey, d-do you want to meet up at the weekend?"

"Yes!" Theodora crowed. "Do you want to come to my house?"

Dexter didn't answer right away.

"Oh," Theodora said softly, thinking Dexter must have heard the rumours about her family. Mummy would be so disappointed – she already had Wilhelmina brewing a new glamour potion just in case (fuzzy cardigan included) – but Theodora was enjoying having a human friend too much to make a fuss.

"I'm sure Dexter would love to go to your house," said Mrs Adebola, eyeing her son with a severe expression that made Theodora feel certain Mrs Adebola wasn't someone to mess with.

"Sure," Dexter agreed in a small voice.

"That's OK, Mrs Adebola," said Theodora quickly. "My house is a bit strange. There are all sorts of rumours about the mansion being haunted, and – well, I understand. Besides, I've got a big family and a pet tarantula and…"

"Wow," Dexter breathed. "I love bugs."

"You'd like Sherman," Theodora said hopefully.

"A pet tarantula?" repeated Mrs Adebola. "How … unusual."

"That's me," Theodora replied. "Unusual."

Something Wicked This Way Comes

Before Dexter arrived for his visit, the inhabitants of 13 Battington Lane scurried about readying the mansion for a human; they would *definitely* be more prepared this time. Marty stationed the cubs in

the playroom, from where their tiny howls couldn't be heard and from where Sylvester couldn't escape. Dracula was attending a meeting at the Paris MLM but had

locked all the bats inside the highest tower so they wouldn't swoop in unexpectedly. Mummy made Theodora clean her room ("But I like it messy!") and also made sure that each and every member of the MLM was glamoured or hiding.

"I will stay in the music chamber this tiiiiiiime," sang Figaro.

"Meow. Meow," agreed Bandit, which probably meant, "Georgie and I will be in my room eating candyfloss and playing the guitar."

"Then we're all set.

And I've baked cupcakes," smiled Mummy, setting a silver, skull-plated tray on the counter.

"Thanks, Mummy," said Theodora, stealthily removing a smattering of sugared slugs from the slime-green frosting when Mummy wasn't looking.

Dexter arrived promptly at four o'clock. Theodora was waiting in the hallway, her freckled nose pressed against the glass windowpanes in the front door. She thought Dexter looked nervous as he made his way up the pumpkin-lined path. His hand shook as it stretched towards the squishy blue eyeball the monsters used in place of a doorbell.

"Hi, Dexter," said Theodora, hastily unlocking the door before he had time to ring it.

"H-hi," he mumbled, cringing at the awful screeching sound the door made as it opened.

"Come on in," she said, stepping aside to let him pass.

"May I take your coat, sir?" asked Helter-Skelter, glamoured to look like a human butler, suddenly appearing at Theodora's side.

"Th-thanks," Dexter stammered, tipping his head back to observe the butler's tall, slim figure and thinking that he looked as if he could use a few square meals.

"So, what do you want to do first?" Theodora asked as Helter-Skelter strode to the coat cupboard. He slid the door sideways, revealing a rack full of lush fur coats, hats and stoles (several of which weren't actually dead – in fact, two arctic foxes and a handful of mink were breathing quite steadily; luckily unnoticed by Dexter). "Want a tour of the house?"

"M-maybe later," said Dexter, eyeing an amethyst umbrella stand covered in rectangular *things* horribly resembling human fingernails.

"Want to meet Sherman? Or we could have a snack? Mummy baked cupcakes."

"Cupcakes s-sound good," said Dexter.

They made their way into the kitchen, where Mummy, dressed in her new sweater-set and matching headband, was draped over the worktop reading *The Monster Homemaker's Guide to Entertaining* and an apron-clad Wilhelmina was sweating over a boiling cauldron.

"So nice to meet you, Dexter," said Mummy, carefully marking her place in the book and sliding off her stool to greet him.

"N-nice to m-meet you, too."

"And this is Theodora's aunt, Wilhelmina," Mummy continued, gesturing towards the corner of the room, where silver sparks were flashing beneath the witch's bony fingers.

Wilhelmina waved vaguely in their direction and frowned at her concoction. "I forgot the frogs," she muttered under her breath. "You'd think I had no more intelligence than some terrible *hag*. Helter-Skelter?" she called.

Before the words had left her lips, Helter-Skelter
emerged from the pantry lugging a dented metal
bucket filled with some unidentifiable liquid. He
walked slowly so as not to slosh it over the sides,
or to allow any of its occupants – which, based on
the racket coming from its depths ("ribbit", "ribbit"),
were *alive* – to escape.

"Just set them there, please," said Wilhelmina,
nodding towards the butcher's block on her left.
"Ta, Helter-Skelter."

"What's his name?" Dexter asked
Theodora in an undertone.

"Um, Hector-Skeeter," said
Theodora, thinking fast.

"Oh," said Dexter, climbing
onto the stool Mummy had
just vacated. "I thought I heard
something else."

"Who wants cupcakes?" Mummy
offered, placing the platter between them.

"I do!"

"Me too!"

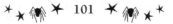

101

"What's this on top?" asked Dexter, nudging the lone slug that had evaded Theodora's icing purge with his finger.

"Nothing," she said quickly. "Here, I'll take it."

But as she reached for it a long, sticky tongue – yes, *tongue* – shot out between them.

"W-what was that?" asked Dexter, snatching his hand away and staring at the slimy thing hopping across the worktop.

"Just a frog," she said, catching it in her cupped hands and running it over to Wilhelmina.

"W-why's there a frog in your kitchen?" Dexter wanted to know as she sat back down.

"Um…" she stalled, picking at the cupcake case and scattering crumbs all over her plate.

"We're having boiled frog's legs for supper," Mummy interjected, squeezing Theodora's shoulder in silent warning to let her do the talking. "They're a French delicacy, you know?"

After their cupcakes (which despite the tangy flavour left by the slugs were actually quite good), they wandered up to Theodora's room to visit

Sherman, who was on his best behaviour. He'd forgone his top hat and monocles (humans have no appreciation of *monster couture*) and didn't utter a single word, though he was sorely tempted when the discussion turned into a debate over who would win in a fight to the death – a tarantula or a scorpion?

"Definitely a tarantula," said Theodora.

The rest of the afternoon went just as smoothly.

Sure, one of the suits of armour might have sneezed as they ambled past, but Theodora didn't think Dexter had noticed – she'd covered it with a fake cough of her own. And yeah, a couple of eyes in the staircase had blinked in surprise at the sight of a human who wasn't Theodora (for all her efforts, Mummy had forgotten to warn the *mansion* about their guest). And fine, if we're really being honest, there *was* one very tense moment when a dozen frogs making a cauldron-break went zooming over the tops of Dexter's shoes, followed by an irate Wilhelmina shouting about her ruined potion. ("She means soup," Theodora hastily corrected.)

But otherwise it was fine.

Yes, all in all, things were going well for Theodora. She'd made a human friend. She'd avoided another run in with Ms Frumple. And no more earwax had appeared at the mansion or at school. Later, Theodora would tell Sherman she should have known it was too good to last.

And I must say, she really should have – the cards had been warning her, after all.

The past – *The Lady*, mystery.

The present – *The Castle*, danger.

The future – *Death*, demise.

Most alarmingly, the cards were still behaving strangely. Well, two of them were. The black bird – a mere speck just a few days before – now took up a quarter of *The Castle* card. The *Death* card, too, was altered, a cloaked figure appearing behind the Grim Reaper, though it was too small for them to see properly (but probably not for long). Only *The Lady* remained unchanged.

"I've never heard of such a thing," Sherman fretted, clicking his pincers together.

"Stop worrying," said Theodora, who was too

pleased with the way everything else was going to get worked up. "They must be magic. Georgie probably just forgot to mention it."

"But they've never changed before – why now?"

Theodora shrugged.

"Incidentally, you haven't seen any black birds around, have you?" As Sherman spoke, the bird on the card grew before their very eyes, its beak curving cruelly, its talons elongating, its feathers darkening.

"Erm, I don't think so," Theodora said, avoiding both the card and Sherman's probing gaze (lying to Sherman was almost as bad as lying to Mummy, but he'd have been so worried – unnecessarily so – if Theodora had told him that she had, in fact, seen a large black bird).

And so Theodora ignored the cards' warnings, and it wasn't until Dexter's second visit, the following weekend, that she realized her luck was about to change. And not for the better.

They'd just finished playing Monopoly in the Games Room (which held a pool table, a card table and more board games than Theodora could count –

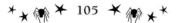

it was *awesome*). Marty, disguised as a car salesman, wandered into the room. He sat on a blue velvet chaise longue and pulled a bone – the kind you'd give to a dog – out of his trouser pocket. He began polishing it with a hanky, as if this was as normal as cleaning a pair of reading glasses.

As the bone began to gleam, Bandit sauntered into the room, stalking over to where Theodora and Dexter were sitting on the rug. He plopped down smack in the middle of the board, scattering the little houses everywhere. As their game had just ended, this wasn't a particularly big deal.

What *was* a big deal was that he leapt to his feet a few seconds later, hacking and shuddering as if he was coughing up a hairball. Unfortunately, what came spewing out of Bandit's mouth wasn't a clump of fur, but one – no, two – no, *three* – vampire mice. Drenched in stomach juices but otherwise unharmed, they tottered around in drunken circles, clutching their aching heads.

"Are those m-mice?" asked Dexter, looking down at the critters in equal parts horror

and disgust. "Did your cat just spit up *live* m-mice?"

"Um…"

Before Theodora could think up an excuse, she heard a loud crunching sound emitting from the blue velvet chaise longue. Or rather, *Marty* was emitting a loud crunching sound: he was gnawing on the bone.

Yes, gnawing. Like a dog. Or a wolf.

"Is your u-uncle *chewing on a bone*?" asked Dexter, his mouth hanging open.

"Erm…" Theodora might have been able to smooth things over entirely. In fact, she nearly did – she managed to convince Dexter that the mice were just wind-up toys (they scampered into a mouse hole before he could check if this was true) and that Marty wasn't actually eating a bone, but an oversized lollipop moulded into the shape of one.

"They're from Sweden," Theodora invented wildly, pulling Dexter from the Games Room. "I'll see if he can bring some back for us on his next business trip."

Yes, she almost got away with it. That is, until they bumped into Bon.

They were heading into the kitchen for a snack.

Theodora was only half listening to Dexter's chatter about the upcoming Chess Club tournament. Even so, she was just trying to mind her own business – she certainly wasn't *looking* for trouble – but as she passed Dracula's study she noticed the door was ajar. As monsters aren't very good at remembering to close doors, this was not unusual. What *was* unusual was Bon sitting on top of his desk.

"That's strange," Theodora murmured, wandering into the study. "What are you doing down here? This, er, stuffed animal is usually kept in the guest room," she added for Dexter's benefit.

Bon, of course, was under strict orders from Mummy not to speak in front of the human boy and could not respond.

"T-that's a weird looking toy," said Dexter, joining Theodora at the desk. "Wait, did … did it just blink?"

"No," Theodora said quickly. "Of course not."

But Theodora was staring hard at Bon; she'd seen it too. The bonadoo might be a bit of a rebel, but he would never openly disobey Mummy – not after all those years in reform school (seven, if you must know). And since Theodora was certain Mummy wouldn't have given Bon permission to come down from the third floor while Dexter was over, she figured it had to be something major for the bonadoo to break direct orders.

There was a creaking sound as Bon moved his paw slightly, shifting it onto a piece of paper Theodora hadn't initially noticed.

"D-did that s-stuffed animal just move?"

"Course not," Theodora repeated, not really paying attention. She snatched the paper – an envelope – off the desk.

Now here's where Theodora got herself into trouble (you would have too). She ripped the envelope open, unfolded the letter inside and began to read it.

I know what you're thinking: she definitely wasn't minding her own business, taking a letter from someone's desk and reading it. No wonder she got into trouble! Did I mention that the words scrawled across the envelope in cramped, uneven writing read, *Regarding Theodora*?

See, I told you. You'd have done the same thing if you'd seen a letter with your name on it.

Smoothing the paper, Theodora read what was written there.

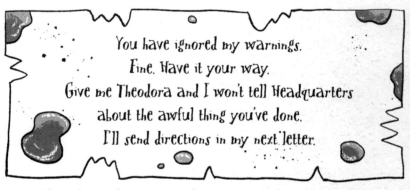

You have ignored my warnings.
Fine. Have it your way.
Give me Theodora and I won't tell Headquarters about the awful thing you've done.
I'll send directions in my next letter.

Theodora's heart was thumping in her chest. She could scarcely breathe. "When did this letter arrive? Today?"

Bon nodded, moving his head ever so slightly.

"Did Owen drop it off?"

Another almost imperceptible nod.

"Theodora," said Dexter, frantically pulling on the sleeve of her sweater. "That s-stuffed animal is moving – I'm sure of it!"

"Not now, Dexter. I've got to think."

She flipped the letter over in her hand, looking for clues. There, in the corner. An inkblot, like the kind made by an old fountain pen. And…

"Earwax," she breathed.

"Theodora, Mrs Adebola is here!" Mummy called from the other room.

"Coming!" came Theodora's sing-song reply. She quickly shoved the letter into the crumpled envelope. She placed it back on the desk, trusting that Bon would rearrange it after she'd left. "You won't tell anyone I opened it, will you?"

Bon shook his head infinitesimally to the left, then the right, ears flapping against his mane.

Theodora breathed a sigh of relief. "Thank you. Ready, Dexter? Dexter?"

But Dexter wasn't in the study.

"We're in the Beelzebub Parlour," Mummy yelled.

Theodora hurried into the parlour (they had four, one of which Theodora was never allowed to enter, though no one would explain *why* – grown-ups do like their secrets, don't they?), a massive room with a great stone fireplace perfect for roasting marshmallows, heavy crimson drapes that blocked the wintery draught and cloying summer heat alike, and a high ceiling featuring intricate wooden carvings of devils and sprites.

"It seems Dexter's having an asthma attack," Mrs Adebola was explaining to Mummy. "Luckily I have his inhaler with me. You really should start remembering to carry it yourself, Dex. You're old enough now."

"Is he going to be OK?" Theodora asked worriedly.

"Yes, this happens sometimes. Too much pollen in the air. Or if he was—"

"S-scared," Dexter choked out.

Mrs Adebola frowned. "Did something frighten you?"

"Creepy s-stuffed a-animal."

Mummy's eyes widened. "A stuffed animal?" she

repeated, twisting the strand of pearls at her neck, eyes darting over to Theodora, who'd gone rather pale.

"It was m-moving."

"Nonsense!" said Mrs Adebola swiftly. "Toys don't move on their own."

"And the c-cat spat up *live* mice, and a m-man was chewing on a *bone*," he continued, teeth chattering. "And l-last time a l-lady was brewing a potion and the stairs were m-moving…"

"Dexter, have you been reading horror novels again?" asked Mrs Adebola sharply. "I told your father those books were too scary."

"N-no."

"Hmm," said his mother in a disbelieving tone. She turned towards Mummy, still keeping one eye on her son. "Thank you for a wonderful afternoon. Same time next week?"

Without waiting for a reply, Mrs Adebola steered Dexter out of the house, Theodora waving miserably after them.

The Plan

This is the point in our story when things started to go very badly – no, terribly – no, horribly – for Theodora. And not horribly like when you scrape your knee or lose a sock. I mean horribly like when you wake up with a stiff neck on the wrong side of the bed and put your clothes on backwards before falling down the stairs on your way to a breakfast of lumpy porridge, forgetting to wear your wellies and having to spend the whole day in smelly wet socks.

It all started when Dracula found the torn letter on his desk. Deciding there was no time to lose, he didn't run to gather the others for an emergency meeting – he *flew*. With a swish of his cape he was gone, a dozen furry bats appearing in his place. Being able to split yourself twelve ways came in handy at times such as this. They dispersed in a flurry of wings, each tasked with locating a member of the MLM and bringing him or her to the mausoleum.

"What's the meaning of this, Dracula?" demanded Sir Pumpkin-de-Patch half an hour later. "I was tending to the pumpkins. Halloween's coming and they need constant attention."

"They'll be fine, Pumpkinhead," Marty growled. "They're plants. The cubs, on the other hand, are in the playroom unsupervised…"

The monsters winced.

Before he found himself with a mutiny on his hands, Dracula quickly filled everyone in on the arrival of the second earwax-coated letter.

"But who would do such a thing?" Mummy cried.

"What is it, exactly, that this – *individual* – is planning to tell Headquarters?" wondered Wilhelmina. "We've done nothing wrong!"

"We've done one thing wrong," Grimeny Cricket countered quietly, eyes straying towards the bottom of the MLM Charter, where the fourth rule – the one about not letting anyone discover that Theodora was living at the mansion – had been added almost ten years earlier.

The monsters shifted uncomfortably, avoiding each other's guilty gazes.

"I'd better fly to Headquarters and try to sort this out," Dracula decided. "Georgie, can I trust you to beef up security in my absence?"

"Eurgggg," confirmed Georgie. Bandit nodded sanctimoniously at his side.

Four more gargoyles were added to the roof, reporting to Bob and Sally. Extra bats were flown in to man the towers. Bandit was to patrol the perimeter hourly, and even the Headless Horseman consented to leave his haunted forest to guard the gates. Sherman was given a special whistle and told not to hesitate to use it at the first sign of anything

unusual and *not* to tell Theodora about it (he told her immediately, of course). And, as a precaution, the monsters were taking turns following Theodora.

I know what you're thinking, and I agree – what an invasion of privacy! But in the monsters' defence, it was clear that the letter writer, whoever he-she-or-it was, wanted Theodora. And as the monsters had no intention of handing her over, they feared the letter writer might take drastic measures. What if he-she-or-it tried to kidnap her? Better to invade Theodora's privacy than risk losing her, they reasoned.

Most unusually, Theodora didn't make a fuss when she realized this. Nor did she make a peep when one of the new gargoyles refused to let her inside the mansion.

("Mate, that's who we're trying to protect – let her in, for darkness' sake!") And she stayed silent as the grave – a poor analogy, perhaps, given that we know some graves have a great deal of activity, but you get the gist – when glamoured monsters kept showing up at school to check on her.

"You forgot your lunch," said Mummy. (She hadn't.)

"You forgot your house key," said Wilhelmina. (It was in Theodora's pocket.)

"The cubs – er, kids – missed you," said Marty. (This, she suspected, was true.)

What's that? You're wondering why Theodora tolerated this?

The answer is simple.

Theodora had a plan – a good one. But she was afraid that if she mentioned any of the recent goings-on she might let something slip – the words would tumble out of her mouth faster than snot falling out of Billy Ellis's nose – and everything would be ruined.

Her plan? It was simple.

Theodora was going to intercept the next letter (she was still working out how, but where there's a will there's a way, and Theodora certainly didn't lack will), and then she was going to hand herself over to whomever – or *whatever* – was after her. Though, if she was being perfectly honest, the thought of it made her stomach churn.

But perhaps she was getting ahead of herself. It was possible the letter writer meant no harm; maybe he-she-or-it was a stout observer of the MLM Rules and simply couldn't abide the idea of a human living among monsters, no matter that it would break Theodora's heart into a million pieces to be separated from her family. Yes, perhaps the letter writer was well meaning, if a little misguided, and just wanted to send Theodora to a nice, normal, *boring* human family...

But what if the letter writer had more sinister intentions? What if he-she-or-it thought Theodora was dangerous, a *living* threat to the Monster Secrecy Act, whose very existence risked exposing monsters to humans? What if the letter writer wanted to make her, well, *un*-living?

Theodora gulped. *Maybe it wouldn't be so bad*, she reasoned. Perhaps she could return as a vampire, or a zombie. Or she supposed it wouldn't be too awful to be a ghost, though she'd dearly miss eating pizza.

I know what you're thinking. It's all over your face like a rash or chocolate or lipstick left by your Great Aunt Ruth when she gives you a big, wet kiss and you put up with it because she slips you a five pound note or because your mum will kill you if you don't. You're thinking, "Is Theodora crazy? Why would she turn herself over to some clearly dangerous individual who wants to tear her away from her family – or *worse*?"

Theodora would tell you there were several reasons.

Firstly, she loved her family more than anything. She couldn't bear the thought of something bad happening to them (and getting reported to Headquarters *definitely* counted as something bad – from what Sherman had told her, there were very severe punishments for rule breaking). If it was within her power to protect them, then that was what she was going to do.

Secondly, Theodora was not the type of person who was content to sit at home and wait for whatever was chasing her to catch up. She'd much rather face things head-on.

And thirdly, she had a funny feeling that *she* was the "awful thing" the MLM had done. She'd been staring at the three rules (of course, she didn't know there was a fourth, given that it was written in invisible ink) listed on the MLM Charter for as long as she could remember. And what was the very first rule?

Keep monsters hidden from humans.

Obviously, they'd broken that rule when they adopted her. She supposed someone had figured it out and was using her to hurt the MLM, though she couldn't imagine why anyone would want to do so.

"They'll never give me up," Theodora was telling Sherman over a slice of pumpkin pie they'd snuck into her room.

"I should think not," Sherman blustered, liberally

applying strawberry jam to his half. "You're part of the family."

"We've got to get the next letter before the MLM does."

Sherman grew very quiet. He was thinking so deeply, his pincers weren't even clicking. "Um, Theodora?" he asked after several minutes had ticked past and Theodora had nearly finished her portion. "You're not going to do anything, well, *stupid*, are you?"

"Like what?"

"Like hand yourself over to the letter writer?"

She didn't answer.

"Theodora, I cannot allow—"

"Allow? *Allow?* You can't tell me what to do, Sherman," she said, reddening. "You're not in charge of me!"

"Of course not," said Sherman, beginning to sweat. (Can tarantulas sweat?) "But what if you give yourself to the letter writer and he comes after the MLM anyway? Then you'll have put yourself in peril for nothing."

"Just stop it!" Theodora cried, covering her ears with her hands. "If you're not going to help me, just get out of here."

"Of course I'll help you," said Sherman, his eight milky eyes filling with tears behind his monocles.

"I'm so sick of everyone always telling me what to do!" Theodora said, slamming her fork onto the now empty plate. "I thought you, of all monsters, would understand!"

Sherman didn't reply.

Theodora didn't notice; she was too busy staring out of the window, where the Headless Horseman was riding his great black stallion, keeping a lookout for whatever was after her. Flames flared from the horse's nostrils each time its hooves hit the dirt, as if in protest at the task; stallions made of fire and sinew were not content to trot along the same small stretch of land – they were made to *run*. Theodora understood the feeling. She'd had enough of being locked away in the mansion, unable to even play in her own back garden. "I won't take it any more, Sherman," she declared.

And still Sherman didn't respond.

She turned back towards the bed. "Sherman?"

But the room was Sherman-less.

"Sherman?" she repeated, to no avail: the tarantula was gone, having scuttled up the wall, disappearing into a crack in the ceiling. "I'm sorry," she said to the empty room. Her shoulders sagged, the pie sitting as heavy as a boulder in the pit of her stomach. "Sherman," she tried again, moving to stand directly beneath the crack in the ceiling. "Did you hear me? I'm sorry!"

But there was no reply.

And, I am sorry to say, if Theodora thought things were going to get any better the next day, she was sorely mistaken. In fact, things were about to get much, much worse.

The Crow

Dexter was avoiding Theodora. She was nearly certain of it. He wouldn't catch her eye during class – not even when Billy picked his nose and wiped it under his desk or when Mrs Dullson spilled coffee down her blouse after giving Billy a proper telling-off. He didn't offer to swap his snack for her (undoubtedly) more interesting one. He wasn't at lunch (Theodora suspected he was hiding in the nurse's office). And he was noticeably absent from Chess Club.

Theodora was the first to enter the classroom that Monday afternoon. She made a beeline for their usual desk and began setting up the board, glancing at the door each time it opened. But to her dismay Dexter was not among the students trickling into the room in twos and threes. And when Ms

Frumple called the club to order and Dexter still hadn't appeared, Theodora was forced to accept he wasn't coming.

More troubled by this than she cared to admit, she snatched the pieces off the board, shoving them into the felt pouch in which they were stored. A shadow fell across the desk as she grabbed another handful.

"No Dexter today?" asked Ms Frumple.

"I don't think so," Theodora replied, trying – and failing – to keep the disappointment out of her voice.

"That's too bad," said Ms Frumple, an ugly smile twisting her thin, colourless lips.

Theodora shrugged, dropping the board and the pouch into their cardboard box. She replaced the cover with a sort of finality; she didn't think she'd be playing again any time soon.

She stood, pulling her yellow raincoat from the back of her chair. A glance at the window confirmed she was going to need it, as thick streams of water gushed down the sides of the glass. She frowned; *of course* it was raining (forget cats and dogs, more like tigers and wolves). It was a perfectly terrible end to a perfectly terrible day. And that was *before* Theodora saw something that made the skin on her arms prickle into gooseflesh…

It was the crow, returned to its perch in the window, just barely visible through the downpour. Now, you might be wondering why Theodora was so convinced it was the same bird. Surely this crow didn't look so different from any other. Aren't they all roughly the size of small chickens? Don't they all have scaly feet and razor-sharp beaks?

You're right, of course. All crows are roughly the same size and have similar features. But they do *not* all have eyes the colour of raw carrots. That *particular* characteristic was unique.

A sudden clap of thunder boomed overhead, causing Theodora to jump. There was a flash of lightning, momentarily illuminating the gloomy classroom. But Theodora did not register this change in atmosphere; she had eyes only for the crow. And in the brief instant the room lit up like a Christmas tree, Theodora saw something very strange indeed…

The crow no longer appeared to be a living, breathing bird, but the *skeleton* of one long dead. Its feathers had vanished. The scaly skin of its feet was gone. Even the carroty irises had disappeared, leaving behind empty, gaping eye sockets.

Theodora gasped; she knew what this was. No wonder the bird's presence made her so uneasy – it wasn't *actually* a bird. The creature huddled on the windowsill was no fowl, but *foul*; it was a skele-crow.

You want to know what a skele-crow is? I should think it was rather obvious, but just so we're all on the same page (p. 130), I'll explain: a skele-animal is a skeletal monster who can take the fleshy form of any animal, in this case a crow.

Ah, you're wondering why he chose to reveal himself? I don't think it was intentional. In fact, I'm sure he would've been in big trouble if it came to be known that he had (and not just with Headquarters). No, I think *that* was accidental.

You see, the only thing that can compel a skele-animal to reveal its true nature is light, the enemy of all that blossoms in the dark. A ray of sunshine, the beam of a flashlight, a strike of lightning – any and all will do.

Anyway, Theodora wasn't surprised that a monster had appeared at school (as you now know, monsters can be found *everywhere*). What she *was* surprised by was the fact that the skele-crow seemed to be alone. This was most uncommon, as they usually paired up with other monsters. Recalling the earwax coated letters delivered to the MLM and the trail of earwax she and Dexter had discovered at school, Theodora couldn't help wondering if perhaps there *was* another monster around. A bigger, stronger monster. One whose ears were dripping with wax…

Before Ms Frumple could tell her not to, she'd bolted from the classroom, down the corridor and through the metal doors that led to the playing field. Splashing through puddles and sliding on slippery leaves, she skidded to a stop in front of the window from which she had spied the skele-crow.

She was too late. It was gone.

Theodora sighed. She was about to head home when something caught her eye. She took a step closer to the windowsill. There was something there.

Something yellow.

Something sticky.

It was earwax, a thick sludge of it glommed onto the narrow ledge.

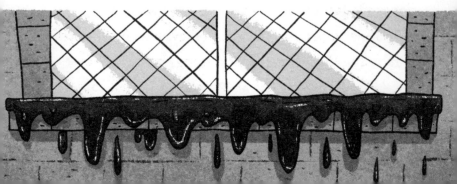

"May I ask what you're doing?"

Theodora turned sharply. It was Ms Frumple.

"Well?" she prompted, her face half-shielded by the edge of her umbrella.

Before Theodora could utter a response, Ms Frumple was dragging her back into the school. They stopped just inside, dripping onto Mr Jackson's freshly waxed floors.

"Now," said Ms Frumple, releasing Theodora and shaking out her umbrella before placing it upside down to dry. "What were you doing?"

"Nothing."

"You were standing outside an Appleton Primary classroom *in the rain*. Why?"

"I … I…" Theodora wracked her brains for a suitable response. "I saw a crow through the window … and I was afraid it might get swept away in the storm … so … I just went to check on it."

"I saw no crow," said Ms Frumple, frowning.

"That's because it had already flown away," said Theodora earnestly. "It was gone by the time I got there."

"A likely story," snapped Ms Frumple. "What were you *really* doing?"

Before Theodora could insist she was telling the truth, Mr Jackson shuffled into the corridor dragging a suds-filled bucket and well-used mop. He reddened as he caught sight of the filthy water pooling around Theodora and the muddy tracks marking the formerly pristine floor. "Mess and muck!" he cried. "I have half a mind to quit right here an' now."

"No need for that, Mr Jackson," said Ms Frumple swiftly. "You have a mop right there. Surely you can get this cleaned in a jiffy…"

Mr Jackson's face went from red to purple. "That took me hours, that did!"

Taking advantage of Ms Frumple's momentary distraction, Theodora slipped back into the rain, unnoticed – or so she thought.

But Ms Frumple was not so easily deflected. Her frown deepened as she watched Theodora scurry away like a mouse, or a rat – some sort of rodent. "And rodents need to be exterminated," Ms Frumple muttered to herself. "Or, at the very least, removed from my school."

The skele-crow, who was perched just outside the doors, silently agreed: Theodora needed to be taken far, far away from this small, squat building. And she would be – sooner than she could have imagined.

Sneaking, Snaking, Snooping

Theodora decided she wasn't going to tell anyone about the earwax and the skele-crow reappearing at school. Although truthfully, she knew that would have been the right thing to do.

Then why didn't she do it? Why didn't she just confide in Mummy? For the same reason she hadn't earlier: she was afraid she'd jeopardize her plan.

Besides, the increased security around the mansion was already a nuisance; it was bad enough the new gargoyles kept forgetting who she was ("Mate, *how many times* do I have to tell you?") and that Bandit was on duty so often that the garden was now overrun with vampire mice ("My poor pumpkins!"). But if the MLM found out that the letter writer's signature earwax had appeared at

Theodora's school *again* – and the skele-crow with it? Forget it. She'd never have another moment's peace, and then how would she look for clues?

Oh, yes, Theodora was looking for clues. As far as she was concerned the only good thing to come out of these new developments was that she was more determined than ever to catch the letter writer – which is how she ended up snooping around Dracula's office. Again.

What's that? Hadn't she learned her lesson the last time? I think it goes without saying that she had not.

So at nine-fifteen that evening, when the MLM was officially in session (they were now meeting several times a week to compare notes on their efforts to catch the evasive letter writer), instead of watching the werewolf cubs as she normally did (she had begged to be let off, citing a headache), Theodora tiptoed out of her room, crept down the hall, skipped down the ivory staircase and walked right into Dracula's office.

Or at least, she *would* have, if the door hadn't been locked.

"The one time he remembers!" she muttered crossly.

Now, most people would have taken this as a sign they should give up. They would have turned around, marched back upstairs and gone to bed. Theodora, of course, was not so easily discouraged. Besides, it just so happened she knew how to get into the office – or any room in the mansion – whether it was locked or not.

Theodora crossed the kitchen, her footsteps muffled by the fuzzy zombie-bunny slippers (another gift from Georgie) on her feet. She cut through the pantry, down the mirrored hallway and into The Room of Veracity, which housed the talking animal heads, now fast asleep. Had she been paying closer attention, she'd have noticed that the picture of the troll was missing from the Wall of Shame, the patch of silk on which it had hung now several shades lighter than the rest of the fabric. Only the hag's portrait remained.

Without waking the heads to ask for permission, Theodora grazed her fingers against the tear in the silk. The small, rounded door emerged. She'd just

grabbed hold of the doorknob
when a reedy voice asked,
"Going somewhere?"

Still gripping the tarnished
silver, Theodora turned to find
the rabbit surveying her from
his post. "Yes," she replied. "To
the music chamber."

The rabbit's nose twitched, as if scenting the lie.
"At this hour?"

"Yes … I left a book up there when I visited a few
weeks ago."

"I see," said the rabbit, surveying
her from above.

Theodora wondered if he,
too, was recalling her last visit.
She definitely hadn't been
holding a book, or even a bag
in which a book might have
been hidden. So it was a great
surprise – and relief – when the
rabbit said, "Go on, then."

Theodora scurried across the threshold before he could change his mind. When she finally reached the music chamber, she didn't pause, but continued up the winding steps until they came to an abrupt dead end. Well, it wasn't *entirely* dead – there was something there.

Something large and long and lean.

At first glance it looked like the sort of metal pole commonly seen in fire stations, only thicker. And instead of steel the base was a shimmering copper. The biggest difference, though, was that it was *moving*, rasping down the side of the wall and probing the air like a tentacle.

Theodora didn't even cry for help (who would have heard her if she had? Mind you, that wouldn't have stopped *me* from screaming blue murder). Not even when the thing slithered around her legs and hoisted her into the shadows.

"Theodor-aaa," sighed a voice as old as the wind.

From somewhere above, two brilliant balls of light blinked into existence.

No, they weren't lanterns, or torches, or any such

things. The large, fiery orbs were the eyes of a woman – a woman whose face just happened to be sitting in the head of a massive snake. OK, it wasn't *just* a snake. It was a cobra.

Yes, Theodora was wrapped in the undulating tail of a wosnak, a nearly immortal monster that is half-woman, half-cobra.

What's that? You've never heard of a wosnak? I can't say I'm surprised. They're some of the oldest creatures on earth, their stories long forgotten. The wosnak at the MLM mansion is one of only ten or so remaining in the whole wide world. As such, very few people even know they exist, let alone find themselves lifted ten metres into the air by one.

"Hi, Goldie," Theodora replied, patting the creature's metallic scales in greeting.

"Your purpossssse?" Goldie hissed, tongue flickering between poisonous fangs as long as Theodora's forearms.

"I need a key to Dracula's office."

"I seeee," she breathed, the twin suns of her eyes burning brighter.

Now,

most people – or

monsters, for that matter –

wouldn't be so willing to hand over

a key to someone else's private space. Not unless

there was a very good reason for doing so. Wosnaks,

however, have different views on such matters. They're

perfectly happy to break with convention – for a price.

Now, I should probably mention that wosnaks

are magically powerful creatures with the ability

to grant the requestor anything he or she wishes

(within reason – world peace and eternal youth are

out of the question). I should *also* mention that there

are only two things they'll accept in exchange for

granting wishes: presents and riddles.

"Payyyment?"

"Riddle," Theodora said decisively (she'd tried

offering gifts before but Goldie had deemed them

unacceptable, which isn't all that surprising –

wosnaks are notoriously hard to shop for).

"Verrrry well. Riddle me thisss…

"I am a creature of the night,
by day walking in the light.
Loyal as the faithful dog,
I'll follow you through fire or fog.
My legs are many, long and sleek,
though through my eyes I cannot peek.
Last and now it seems the least,
I'll share that I'm a talking beast."

"Hmm," Theodora mused, "a creature of the night." Well, that could be anything – a monster, a nocturnal animal. "A talking beast … that could be you, or a werewolf – even a person," she added, thinking of Ms Frumple, who was more beastly than any monster she'd ever met.

As the minutes ticked by she found herself wishing that Sherman was there with a longing generally reserved for fresh-out-of-the-oven pizza. He had a mind for puzzles – he'd have solved it by now. Perhaps she'd been foolish to come; now that she thought about it, she realized she had never figured out the answer to one of Goldie's riddles without Sherman's help.

"Sherman," she muttered, the pieces clicking into place. "Sherman! That's it," she cried. "The answer to the riddle is Sherman!"

"Correct," said Goldie, the hood of skin around her face flaring out like a fan. "Where isss the tarantulaaa?"

"I think he's been staying in the mausoleum," Theodora said in a small voice, feeling herself shrink beneath Goldie's baleful gaze. "I … I haven't seen him for a while." She had not, in fact, seen Sherman for nearly a week. It was the longest they'd ever gone without speaking. Theodora was beginning to think that she might have overreacted – just a little bit – yelling at Sherman the way she had. Being able to admit when she was wrong, however, was *not* one of Theodora's finer traits, and so she had yet to seek him out.

The wosnak's blazing eyes seemed to dim. "A ssshame," she whispered. "In trying timesss friendsss are sssso important…"

Theodora's stomach clenched, and not only

because she was missing Sherman worse than ever. "Are these trying times, then?" she asked uncertainly.

"The noossse growsss ever tighter."

Theodora wanted to ask what she meant by this, but the wosnak said, "Your rewarrrd!"

An old-fashioned filigree key floated in front of Theodora's nose. She plucked it out of the air, dropping it into her pocket. The next thing she knew, she was being lowered to the floor, the wosnak's tail unwinding itself from her body and scraping its way back up the tower wall.

Her mind buzzing with Goldie's cryptic message, Theodora made her way down the spiral staircase, where the rabbit was waiting.

"I was just about to send someone after you. But Theodora," he said, gaze flitting over her empty hands, "where's your book?"

"It wasn't there after all," she said, reddening. "I must have left it at school." And with that she fled from the room, before the rabbit could ask her any other questions she couldn't – or wouldn't – answer.

Preparations

See, I told you Theodora wasn't easily deterred.
It's impressive, really – not many people would
have gone to so much trouble for a key (especially
considering how often monsters forget to lock doors
to begin with; many of them are so old – ancient,
even – that sometimes they have a hard time
remembering such things).

Checking there was no one around, Theodora
fitted the key into the lock and heard the telltale
click. An instant later the key vanished, leaving a
thin tendril of smoke in its place. Theodora entered
the study, closing the door behind her.

Where to begin?

Bookcases bursting with leather-bound
manuscripts and an odd assortment of knick-

knacks – a powdered wig, a fencing sword, garlic cloves (all that business about vampires hating garlic is complete and utter nonsense; every one I've ever met *loves* Italian food) – stood against one wall. Against the other stood a drinks trolley boasting crystal decanters smelling strongly of something metallic, almost like coins, each filled with a viscous red liquid. (Yes, it was blood. Dracula is something of a connoisseur, collecting vintages from all over the world, including the ever-popular 1962 Type A and the rare, full-bodied 1436 Type O Positive).

Deciding that neither the shelves nor the trolley were likely to hold any clues, Theodora strode towards the desk. It offered only a list (*Pick up dry cleaning, Order new lining for coffin*) and several framed photos (Theodora as a nappy-clad toddler; as a gap-toothed seven-year-old; and, her favourite, blowing out her tenth birthday candles with Mummy). Finding nothing useful on top of the desk, Theodora started opening the drawers. She wasn't exactly sure what she was looking for, but figured she'd know it when she saw it.

It wasn't until she got to the third drawer that she stumbled upon something interesting: a crumpled business card. It was so creased and filthy she could barely read its minuscule print (though she thought she could make out the word "monster"). She flipped it over. On this side there were no words, just four letters: ESMA. Below them was an imprint of a lopsided eye which appeared to have been drawn by someone who wasn't quite sure what an eye was supposed to look like. Theodora pocketed the card and resumed her search.

At last, she discovered her first real clue. Hidden under the flimsy false bottom of the fifth drawer was a piece of parchment bearing a wax seal. It featured the letters "HQ" inside something circular – a chain, or maybe a necklace. If Sherman had been there, he'd have said it resembled a *noose*...

"Headquarters," Theodora murmured, noting the address cramped into the upper left corner of the page (*MLM Headquarters, 666 Devil's Way, Transylvania 7666, Romania, Europe, Earth*). She straightened the paper and read it aloud.

Dear Count Dracula,

We received your letter regarding suspected troll activity. We appreciate your bringing this matter to our attention and share your concern that copious amounts of earwax have been found upon letters addressed to the MLM and in the human village of Appleton. I forwarded your message to the Invisible Man (as you know, he has been researching troll hunting habits in the Highlands), who assures me that all four hundred members of the European Troll Cluster are accounted for. They are currently under house arrest for that distressing incident with the Billy Goats Gruff (we've managed to convince them not to sue).

We have also had the Head Jailer check the Transylvanian Extra-dark, Extra-damp, Extra-dreary Prison. Trollic the Terrible (thank you for sending his portrait – it was most helpful) is still there. However, please advise of any additional earwax instances, or of any other unusual activity, and we will send a representative to investigate.

Yours in darkness, etc,

M. Shelley (personal assistant to Dr Frankenstein)

So the MLM thought the letter writer was a troll too. Theodora wondered if they also suspected the troll was working with another monster as she did – the skele-crow. She supposed they didn't, as there'd been no mention of it in Headquarters' note. The portrait they mentioned must be the painting of Trollic the Terrible that had been missing from the Wall of Shame. That made sense…

"Sylvester, give that back," commanded a voice so deep and mournful it could only belong to Helter-Skelter.

Theodora hastily thrust the letter back into the desk. With a quick glance around to ensure nothing was out of place, she hurried from the room. Out in the hallway, she found Sylvester chewing on something long and white. Helter-Skelter was tugging at the thing's other end, hopelessly trying to wrench it from the cub's locked jaws.

"Helter-Skelter!" Theodora cried, catching a flash of something resembling a hand in the midst of the scuffle. "Is that your *arm*?"

"Yes," he replied through gritted teeth. "He's had it for nearly an hour – it'll be a miracle if it still works – and darkness knows what the other cubs have been up to."

"Sylvester, drop it!" Theodora ordered.

The cub froze, eyeing Theodora warily, but made no move to release the bones.

"Sylvester, drop it. *Now*," she repeated in her sternest, Mummy-est voice.

Sylvester spat out the arm.

"Thank you, Theodora," said Helter-Skelter gratefully, picking up the limb, slick with spittle, and fitting it into his shoulder socket. He wiggled his fingers and swung the arm to and fro, checking that it was still functional (it was).

"No problem. I'm sorry you had to watch the cubs alone. I wanted to help but I had something really important to do – I mean, I had a headache."

"Not to worry, miss," he said, scooping the cub

into his arms (Sylvester immediately began gnawing on his collarbone). "And I wasn't alone. Sherman was with me."

"Oh," said Theodora. She hesitated, then added, "How is he?"

"Looking a bit off colour, actually."

"Really?"

"Yes," he replied knowingly, though Theodora pretended not to notice.

"Do you know where he was headed next?"

"He said something about the library."

"Thanks," she called, already sprinting off down the corridor. Now finding her slippers to be more hindrance than help, she paused to kick them off, then continued barefoot towards the library.

"Hi, Hamlet," she said breathlessly as she approached the skull. "Is Sherman around?"

"'Fraid you just missed 'im," Hamlet replied.

Theodora's shoulders sagged. "Thanks anyway," she murmured, feeling low – no, *lower* than low.

What if Sherman never spoke to her again – what if he avoided her *for ever*? It was bad enough that

Dexter wasn't speaking to her, but Sherman was her oldest, dearest friend – the cheese to her pizza. Being without him was like being without air to breathe; there'd been a terrible tightness in Theodora's chest ever since their fight, as if a fist was squeezing her heart in protest at the tarantula's absence.

"Anything else you needed, miss?"

Theodora shook her head, clearing it. "No," she said. "Actually, do you have any books on trolls?"

"Trolls, miss?"

"Yes, trolls. You know, where they live, what they eat, how to catch one…"

"Mousetrap?"

The raven swooped down from somewhere above, landing with a clatter beside the skull.

"Would you please bring Theodora a book on trolls?"

Mousetrap cocked his head.

"There was an excellent one written by L. Munster in 1963. Let's start there."

The raven took flight, hovering beside the unit on Theodora's left. Pecking a slim paperback off the

shelf, he then deftly caught it in his talons before it fell to the floor. He glided back to Theodora, dropping it neatly into her waiting hands.

"Thanks, Mousetrap."

But he was already gone, alighting on a rafter beneath the dusty domed skylight. As Theodora watched him settle into his nest of shredded newspaper, a troubling thought drifted across her mind: from a distance it was hard to tell that Mousetrap was a raven. He could've been any large black bird – a starling, a jackdaw, a *crow*...

An unwelcome shiver ran down her spine. Clutching the book tightly, she thanked Hamlet and hurried out of the library; she had a lot of reading to do if she was going to catch the troll and put a stop to those awful letters once and for all.

Not to knock Theodora's admirable efforts, but I *do* think she would've been wise to research skele-crows, too. She was soon going to find herself face to face with one, after all.

The Invitation

Theodora was determined to set things right with Dexter. Now that she knew what it was like to have a human friend, *not* having one made her feel a bit, well, lonely. It had been nice having someone to talk to at school; someone who attended the same lessons and did the same homework, and who understood – first hand – how horrible Ms Frumple was. Theodora was going to fix things, one way or another… Sherman might be able to avoid her in the many hiding places at home, but Dexter wouldn't be so lucky at school.

So that morning, when Dexter raised his hand to be excused to go to the toilet, Theodora waited until Mrs Dullson was facing the board and slipped out after him (she only allowed one student to leave at a time, no matter how great the emergency).

"Hi, Dexter," she said, when the door to the boys' toilets opened.

"H-hi, Theodora," Dexter stammered in surprise.

She cut to the chase. "Dexter, are you avoiding me?"

"Of c-course not," he said, eyes sliding towards the door as if he was considering ducking back in.

"Is it because of Bon?"

"W-who?"

"Bon. The stuffed animal that looks like a rabbit and a lion got smashed together."

"He was m-moving," Dexter whispered, eyes widening. "And the frogs … and the mice…" He swallowed hard. "I-I've gotta g-get back to class."

"Dexter, wait," she said. She knew what she had to do: it was time to tell her friend the truth. "What if he *was* moving? What if – what if they *all* were?"

"So the r-rumours are true?" Dexter looked positively petrified.

"I didn't say that," she corrected. "I said, *if.*" She sighed. "Dexter, if I tell you something, will you keep it between us?"

Dexter nodded solemnly.

Before she had the chance to continue, they heard the sound of keys jangling like coins in a pocket.

"Quick, in here!" Theodora said, pulling Dexter into the supply cupboard just next to the toilets.

The jangling grew louder. A moment later, Mr Jackson shuffled by with his mop and bucket. "Dang kids gettin' sick all over the place," he muttered. "Like I don' have enough to do."

They waited until the clinking faded away before checking if the coast was clear. Seeing that it was, they crept out of the cupboard – and not a moment too soon, for the fumes from the cleaning supplies were making Dexter feel dizzy.

"As I was saying," Theodora began, but she was distracted yet again by the appearance of something on the floor. It was a folded piece of paper, yellowed by copious amounts of earwax. She snatched it up and unfolded it, careful not to get the sticky substance on her hands. It said:

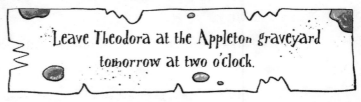

Leave Theodora at the Appleton graveyard tomorrow at two o'clock.

She turned the note over, looking for more to the message, but that was all there was.

But what was that, just there? An imprint scraped into the earwax. She squinted at it, wondering if it might be a stamp or a sticker. Upon closer inspection she saw it was neither; it was a small footprint – or, rather, a three-pronged *talon print*.

The kind a crow might make...

She felt a pull at her sleeve. "Not now, Dexter," she said, still examining the note.

"What are you two doing out of your classroom?"

Theodora froze, stomach sinking like a stone in water. She raised her eyes slowly. To her horror, Ms Frumple was standing before them.

"Just using the toilet," Theodora said innocently, roughly shoving the note into her pocket and smearing earwax all over her hand in the process.

Dexter was too frightened to do more than nod.

"At the same time?"

"I-I have permission from Mrs Dullson, ma'am," Dexter stammered.

"Then, Ms Hendrix, you are out of class without permission?" Before Theodora could respond, Ms Frumple added, "I believe Mrs Dullson only allows *one* student to leave the classroom at a time..." She smiled her horrible crocodile smile. "Detention, Ms Hendrix."

Turning her back to Ms Frumple, Theodora trudged down the corridor, muttering angrily under her breath. Dexter appeared at her side a moment later – it seemed that if he had to choose between her and Ms Frumple he'd choose Theodora, whatever his misgivings.

"And, Mr Adebola!" Ms Frumple called.

The children turned.

"Your hair is looking rather … long," she said, eyeing Dexter's tresses in distaste. "A haircut seems overdue."

"Oh," said Dexter, hanging his head.

Theodora glared at Ms Frumple. "*I* think it looks nice," she said haughtily.

"What you think doesn't count," snapped Ms Frumple. "Back to your classroom, or I shall give you another week's detention for being rude and disrespectful. *Now!*"

Theodora was about to say she didn't really care what Ms Frumple did when she felt Dexter tugging at her sleeve again.

"Leave it," he whispered. "It's not worth it. Trust me."

Theodora disagreed – she thought it was well

worth a week's detention to put the terrible Ms Frumple and her narrow views into place, but she allowed Dexter to lead her back to class.

What a waste, she fumed. She'd landed herself in detention *again* and hadn't even managed to speak to Dexter properly.

But then, as it sometimes does when least expected, inspiration struck.

"Dexter, sit next to me during art, OK? I'll tell you everything – I promise."

"O-OK," he agreed.

That afternoon, Theodora held her paintbrush aloft, then dipped it into a pot of strawberry-red paint. She dabbed at the paper, creating abstract shapes. "You have to pinkie promise not to tell anyone what I'm about to say," she said in a low voice.

"I pinkie promise," Dexter agreed, holding out his little finger. "I swear on pizza!"

Theodora placed her wet paintbrush on the wadded up paper towel at the edge of her painting. They clasped pinkies.

And then she told Dexter everything.

How Georgie and Bandit had found her abandoned in the graveyard as a baby and brought her to live in the mansion. ("Z-zombies eat candyfloss?")

How the monsters had adopted her. ("You mean y-your mom is an *actual* mummy?")

How a series of anonymous letters were threatening to expose the MLM to the rules-obsessed Headquarters in Transylvania. ("How many monster l-leagues *are* there?")

How she'd seen signs of a troll and a skele-crow around school and thought they might be working together to write and deliver the letters. ("Are th-they here now?")

And then a funny thing happened: the ever-present knot in the pit of Theodora's stomach loosened ever so slightly, and she felt better than she had in many days. Better than she had since she'd overheard the owl's report of that first terrible letter.

"S-so your house really *is* haunted, but with g-good monsters?"

"Exactly," said Theodora, picking up her paintbrush.

"Wow," Dexter breathed. "Can I c-come over again soon?"

Happiness swelled in Theodora like a balloon filling with air. "Of course!"

"Theodora, Dexter – less talking, more painting, please."

"Sorry, Mrs Dullson," said Theodora.

But, if Theodora was being honest, she wasn't *actually* sorry: getting reprimanded was a small price to pay to have her friend back. Now, if only she could convince Sherman to talk to her, she thought she would be very happy indeed, *even* knowing that after tomorrow there was a very good chance she'd never see either of them again.

The Graveyard

Theodora was up early the next day despite reading the book Hamlet had chosen for her (*Trolling for Trolls*) until the wee hours of the morning. She had a lot to do to prepare for her two o'clock meeting at the graveyard. (Yes, she was still determined to hand herself over, and, no, she hadn't told the monsters – not even Sherman, whom she feared would sound the alarm with his whistle. Not that she *could've* told him even if she'd wanted to – she still hadn't seen him – and, boy, did she want to.)

In addition to the usual school supplies, Theodora packed a torch, a penknife Grimeny Cricket had given her for her birthday ("Really," Mummy had protested, "she's much too young for such a thing!") and cereal bars. She also threw in a bag of dried herbs, a jar of lavender honey and a strand of Mummy's pearls.

Why did she pack such an odd array of items? Because *Trolling for Trolls* said the best way to catch a troll is to lure it with things it enjoys but has a hard time getting on its own.

Take the dried herbs. Most trolls live under bridges or in seaside caves, so it's very difficult for them to pick fresh herbs, let alone dry them (and a little oregano or sage makes nearly anything taste better – even raw fish or rotted tree stumps, a large part of a troll diet).

Or the honey. Trolls are terrified of bees (they're highly allergic to their stings), so while it's their favourite snack, they're rarely able to eat it.

What about the pearls? Surely they don't eat *jewellery*? Of course they don't. Trolls just like shiny things (they're *literally* gold diggers).

After throwing everything into her bag, Theodora shuffled the torat cards and performed her usual morning reading. As expected, she drew the same three cards.

The Lady: the golden-haired woman offering nothing more than a quizzical smile.

"As usual," Theodora muttered, wondering fleetingly if she'd ever learn the truth about her past.

The Castle: the black bird looming large on the face of the card, eyes lightened from black to orange. There was no mistaking it: it was *her* crow; the crow she'd seen at Chess Club – twice; the crow who'd left a talon print on the last letter; the crow who was really a skele-crow; the crow who, she was certain, was helping the letter writer blackmail the MLM.

Theodora took a deep breath, tossing down the last card.

"*Death*," she murmured. No longer hidden but standing shoulder to shoulder with the Grim Reaper was another cloaked figure, the hood pulled low over its face. Its only distinguishing feature was a claw-like hand clutching a knobbly staff. Theodora assumed it was a troll, though she didn't remember reading that they favoured walking sticks – perhaps this one was elderly?

Deciding there was nothing to do but face whatever was coming, she placed the cards back in their case and threw them inside her brimming rucksack. She went downstairs, ate a breakfast of waffles, and kissed Mummy goodbye.

Now, it goes without saying that we are nearing the most exciting part of our tale; we shall soon be meeting the infamous letter writer.

But first Theodora had to get through the school day.

When she sat down at her desk, she noticed Dexter had had his hair cut: it was now cropped close to his head. It made her sad (and more than a little angry) that Ms Frumple had made him feel bad enough to change it, but she didn't mention it. Neither did Dexter.

Morning stretched into afternoon. Theodora's stomach was beginning to hurt, as if a bunch of snakes was slithering around in there, tying themselves into knots. How was she ever going to manage to sneak out of class and get to the graveyard by two o'clock? Mrs Dullson was watching her like a hawk (on Ms Frumple's orders, Theodora had no doubt). But then an unexpected opportunity presented itself. It was so good – no, clever – no, *ingenious* – Theodora was annoyed she hadn't thought of it herself.

Around one o'clock, an hour before she needed to arrive at the Appleton graveyard, Mrs Dullson announced there would be a test. The class groaned (it was *so* unfair!). They had a feeling it would be on the twelve times table, which had proved more challenging than the eleven and much harder than the ten.

But Billy Ellis, that nose picker, had not yet mastered his nine times table, and had no intention of being tested on his twelve. So he took matters into his own hands.

"Mrs Dullson?" His hand shot into the air. "Can I go to the toilet?"

"I don't know," Mrs Dullson replied with a sniff. "*Can* you?"

"*May* I?" Billy amended.

"You may."

But instead of going towards the toilets, Billy slunk down the hallway, around the corner and into the main corridor. And then he set off the fire alarm.

Now, this worked in Theodora's favour, but you should never, ever pull the fire alarm. Unless, of course, there's a fire. Or if your science teacher is making you dissect a frog. Then it's perfectly fine. (Your parents are upset again, aren't they? They have no sense of humour, these people. I really don't know how you put up with them.)

"OK, class," said Mrs Dullson. "Stay calm. Leave your belongings." Theodora ignored this, hiking her rucksack onto her shoulder. "Line up in single file just as we practised and go to our designated spot on the field by the goalposts."

Of course, the class did no such thing. They flooded into the hallway, merging with the other classes pouring onto the field.

Barely suppressing the grin that had slid onto her face (what an unexpected stroke of luck!), Theodora stepped onto the freshly mown grass, keeping an eye on Mrs Dullson while allowing the crowd to sweep her to the fringes of the group. The teacher wasn't watching, but was attempting to herd the class towards the goalposts (though she'd probably have had better luck herding cats – and *that's* no easy task). Theodora looked left. Theodora looked right. And then she melted into the crowd, slouching off towards the stands where some older kids had gathered. They were rowdy and loud, but Theodora ignored them, and they her. She continued across the field, through the car park and

onto the pavement. Nobody tried to stop her. And before you could say, "This is a bad idea," she was standing outside the graveyard.

The tall iron gates designed to keep visitors out — or, perhaps, to keep the inhabitants *in* — loomed before her. Either way, Theodora knew what she had to do.

She straightened her hair ribbon. She squared her shoulders. And then she pushed the gates open, entering the very place where Georgie and Bandit had found her so many years ago. Now firmly inside, she noticed something strange. The first of many strange things, I'm afraid.

It was as if someone had turned off the sun. Dark, billowing clouds swirled overhead. It was eerily quiet. Not even the wind dared to breathe.

Perhaps it was time to get out her torch, she thought. And maybe Mummy's pearls.

There was a sudden noise.

"W-who's there?" she called.

There it was again – a crunching sound, like someone chewing cereal without any milk added to it.

"Who's there?" she repeated. "Show yourself!"

"It's j-just me," replied a familiar voice.

Theodora squinted into the darkness. "Dexter? Dexter! What're you doing here?"

"I-I saw that note yesterday," he said. "Before Ms Frumple showed up. And I saw you sneak away during the f-fire drill. I tried to tell Mrs Dullson that I thought you might be here, but she wouldn't listen. I was afraid to leave school, but I was more afraid you'd get hurt – ouch!" Dexter cried, as Theodora threw her arms around him.

"You really *are* my friend!" she said.

"Of course I'm your f-friend," he replied, patting

her awkwardly on the back. But Theodora thought he sounded pleased all the same.

"Oh, but I wish you hadn't come. You could get hurt."

"It'll be h-harder for whoever's after you t-to take us both down," said Dexter bravely.

"That's true," Theodora agreed. "Two is better than one."

"And three is better than two," called another familiar voice.

Theodora frowned. "Sherman, is that you?"

"In here."

"I think it's c-coming from your backpack," said Dexter.

Theodora swung her rucksack onto the thistly grass. Crouching, she dragged the zip across the bag. There, top hat perched on his head, was Sherman.

"Sherman!" she cried. "What are *you* doing here?"

"You didn't think I was going to let you come alone, did you?" asked Sherman, adjusting a monocle.

"Even after I yelled at you?"

"Of course. What are friends for? I know you didn't mean it."

"I didn't, and I feel terrible about it. But Sherman, if you knew I didn't mean what I said, why did you run away? I tried to apologize, but you had crawled into the ceiling. I thought you would come back, but you didn't. I thought you were … well, avoiding me."

"I wasn't avoiding you – not exactly. I've been crawling onto your pillow at night after you fall asleep and leaving in the morning before you wake," Sherman said sheepishly. "I was going to apologize when you got home from school today…"

"You don't have anything to be sorry for! I'm the one…"

"… but then that terrible note fell out of your pocket last night," he continued with a shiver.

"Is that how you knew I'd be here? At the graveyard, I mean."

"So, this morning," he continued, as if Theodora hadn't spoken, "before you got up, I hid under the covers, and when you went to the bathroom I crept inside your bag. You nearly squished me with the torch! Though it might be useful. It's a bit dark."

"Did you tell anyone?" asked Theodora worriedly.

"No, I didn't," said Sherman. "I think you're right. Whoever's sending those letters isn't going to stop until they have you … and, well, the thought of never seeing you again … it was too much. I had to come. At least we'll be together, no matter what happens."

"Thank you, Sherman," said Theodora, offering him her hand. He scuttled up her arm, settling on her shoulder. "I'm happy you're here," she added shyly, taking the torch and the penknife out of her bag. "I'd have missed you, too."

Sherman extended a hairy leg towards Dexter, whose mouth was hanging open in astonishment. "Allow me to introduce myself properly," said the tarantula. "I'm Sherman."

"Y-you can t-talk?"

"Of course," Sherman replied. "Though Mummy generally forbids it in front of humans. But I figure the jig is up. Now, has anyone else showed up?"

"Yes," croaked a new, unfamiliar voice. "Someone has indeed."

The three of them jumped at the sudden, frog-like sound. Theodora switched on the torch, sweeping it in an arc across the tombstones. It was no good – as far as she could tell, the cemetery was empty except for the graves and their mouldering occupants.

"Do you see anyone?" she whispered.

"No," Sherman and Dexter replied.

"Over here," said the voice.

They took a few tentative steps forward, leaves crackling under their feet.

"This way," croaked the speaker from somewhere up ahead.

"Sounds like it's coming from over there," said Dexter, pointing towards the middle of the cemetery where the words of mourning engraved upon the oldest stones were no longer legible, washed away by a thousand rainstorms.

They headed that way, beneath the sightless gaze of a towering statue of an avenging angel, sword raised in her marble hand as if poised to strike. Theodora switched open her penknife, holding it tightly in her fist. A pair of yellow eyes glittered in the darkness as they passed the weathered plot of *George Hendrix.*

"Careful, now," Theodora murmured, gazing warily at the eyes. "We don't know what we're dealing with yet."

But the creature, whatever it was, made no move towards them.

"A bit further," prodded the voice. "Behind *Edward the Confessor*."

They were just a few metres away when Theodora came to a halt. She pressed the penknife into Dexter's hand, carefully pointing the blade away from his fingers. "Stay behind me, OK? If anything happens, go straight to the MLM."

Dexter nodded, looking frightened but determined. He adjusted his grip on the knife, readying himself for whatever was coming next.

"We will," Sherman promised, patting Theodora's shoulder before scurrying to Dexter's.

Theodora took a deep breath and stepped forward to meet her would-be kidnapper.

"Theodora," said the voice. "My, how you have grown."

"Do I know you?"

"Certainly," came the reply. "Of course, you haven't seen me in many, many years. Not since that wretched mummy banned me from the MLM. *You've failed in your rehabilitation*," said the voice in a crude imitation of Mummy's Egyptian accent. "*You must go back to reform school or leave.* As if she has any say over what I do! As if I was going to sit

through those wretched lessons again!"

"Who are you?" asked Theodora, wracking her brain for the list of monsters who'd left the MLM over the years. There weren't many.

"I've been called many names," the voice tittered. "But you may call me…"

The Mighty MLM

"… Hilda."

A short, stout woman stepped out from behind a cracked tombstone. She had wiry chin-length hair and a wart on the tip of her crooked nose. She held a familiar-looking, knobbly walking stick in one hand. A skele-crow sat atop it, glaring at them maliciously … a skele-crow with bright orange eyes…

Hilda. There was something familiar about that name. For that matter, there was something familiar about *her*. In fact, Theodora realized, she'd looked at the hag's face on an almost daily basis for the past ten years; it was featured on the Wall of Shame, alongside the now-absent portrait of the troll.

"There was a hag named Hilda…" she began.

"Quite right," said Hilda happily.

182

"But Mummy said you left to join another league," Theodora said uncertainly. "She never said anything about you being *made* to leave…"

"*Mummy*," the hag harrumphed in disdain.

"Hilda – Ms Hag," Theodora began, "are *you* the one who's been writing all those awful letters?"

"Awful? I thought they were rather clever."

So Theodora had been wrong: the letter writer *wasn't* a troll, but a hag. At least she'd been right about the skele-crow. That was something, she supposed.

"But why?" asked Sherman. "Why would you do such a thing?"

"Because that mummy deserves what's coming to her! All her talk of following the rules – imagine my shock when I found out she'd broken the most important rule of all! Last I'd heard she was going to return you to your own kind…"

"But you wouldn't have told Headquarters about me, would you?" demanded Theodora. "They would send me to live with humans!"

"Oh, I never intended that," Hilda said, tapping

her long, fungus-filled nails on her cane. "No, I would never send you to live with mortals. I'm not cruel, you know."

"I'm sorry," said Theodora, shaking her head, "but I don't understand."

"Why, you're going to live with me, dearie."

"*What?*" asked Theodora, a feeling of dread washing over her like a wave.

"Yes," replied Hilda, stroking her chin, from which several black spiky hairs sprouted. "It'll be lovely. Back in the old days, hags kept children as pets, you know. Before that wretched mummy and

that wretched Headquarters signed that wretched treaty with those wretched humans and took the fun out of everything! Forcing monsters to go into hiding when we're *by far* the superior species – the gall of it! If I had my way, I'd bin that rubbish Monster Secrecy Act and monsters would come out into the open and rule the world! And I *will* have my way in the end," she added in a whisper. "But first things first. I've got a nice little cage for you, dearie…"

"And what if I refuse?" challenged Theodora. Her voice was firm, though her insides felt like jelly – jiggly and wiggly and *un*firm.

The skele-crow cawed in rebuke, ceasing only when the hag shushed him.

"Oh, I don't think you'll do that."

Theodora's chin jutted forward. "And why not?"

She caught a flicker out of the corner of her eye. It was Sherman, fiddling with his not-so-secret emergency whistle. Theodora hoped he wasn't thinking of doing anything stupid, like blowing it. She didn't think Hilda or the skele-crow would take too kindly to their drawing attention to themselves.

"Because then I shall tell Headquarters how the MLM broke their most sacred rule in adopting you. And then all your little monster friends will rot in the cold, dank prisons of Transylvania until their trial. And when they're found guilty – which they most certainly will be – well ..." Hilda flashed her yellowed teeth. "... let's just say it won't be pretty."

Theodora thought hard about what Hilda was saying. The hag might be lying – Theodora had no idea how the monster justice system worked – but if even a bit of what she said was true...

"OK," she said in a final sort of way. She gulped,

swallowing the lump in her throat; she would *not* let the wicked hag see her cry. "I'll do it. I'll go and live with you."

"Wonderful!" said the hag, clapping her gnarled hands together.

"But you have to swear you'll never bother the MLM again."

"Of course, of course," said Hilda smoothly. "Come here, dearie. I've got a nice new lead for you. Pink."

"Theodora hates pink," said Sherman waspishly. "And she's not going anywhere."

"Says who?"

"Says us."

Stepping out from behind the statue of the avenging angel was Mummy.

And she wasn't alone.

I know what you're thinking. Seriously, you've got to learn to control your facial expressions if you're ever going to be a … never mind. You're thinking there's going to be some sort of showdown between the good monsters and the bad monsters, aren't you?

You
would be
correct.

"*You*," Hilda hissed,
surveying Mummy with
something like hatred.

"Not just me."

A pair of yellow eyes flashed
beside her, the same yellow eyes
that had watched them from Georgie's grave.

It was Bandit. And where Bandit went…

"Eurggg," Georgie rumbled, his rotting eyes
staring daggers at Hilda as he lumbered over.

"Well, well, well," Hilda drawled. "The dopey
zombie and his loyal feline companion. I must say,
Mummy, you're losing your touch. You certainly
didn't bring the A-team."

Bandit hissed, ears pinned back on
his head, fur standing on end.

"Mummy!" Theodora cried. "How did
you know we were here?"

"Sherman, of course. And we'll be having a chat

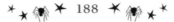

about keeping secrets. I am *not* pleased."

"I thought you said you didn't tell,"
Theodora admonished Sherman in a loud
whisper.

"I didn't," Sherman quipped. "As soon
as I saw Hilda I recognized her from the
Wall of Shame, so I blew the emergency
whistle a few times to alert the MLM."

"B-but I didn't hear a whistle," said Dexter,
finding his voice for the first time in many minutes,
his eyes round as saucers as he took in the sight of
the assembled monsters.

Did I mention they weren't glamoured? There
simply hadn't been time for Wilhelmina to brew the
potions, and the monsters hadn't dared to wait once
they heard the alarm. You can imagine the shock
poor Dexter was feeling as he looked upon
the decrepit Georgie, the bandage-
wrapped Mummy and the *fang*tastic
Bandit. But he was in for an even
bigger surprise...

"That's because it's a

special high-pitched whistle that can only be heard by dogs and—"

"Werewolves," Theodora supplied, putting two and two together.

"Oh, my," Dexter murmured faintly, as Marty took his place beside Mummy. It was one thing to *know* about monsters, but it was quite another to *see* them – especially so many.

"Hi, Marty," said Theodora. "Where are the cubs?"

"Shredding Mummy's new curtains, actually. Left them with Pumpkinhead and you know how nervous he gets around teeth… I'll buy you new ones," he added.

"That's quite all right," said Mummy. "Helter-Skelter will be able to patch them up. Besides, curtains are a small price to pay for our Theodora."

"A very small price indeed." And there was Grimeny Cricket, hopping from headstone to headstone.

"What a lovely reunion," Hilda simpered. "I do so miss the old days when we'd gather round discussing how we'd stop *bad* monsters from attacking people, how we'd teach them to be *good*, how we'd keep ourselves off the humans' radar... I *don't* think!"

"Eurg," growled Georgie, waving his arms. "Eurga-eurg."

"You're right," said Mummy. "Hilda's in desperate need of reform school. Again."

"Never!" cried the hag. "Never again shall I submit to such foolishness! And I'm not alone – darkness, no," she breathed, a fanatical glint creeping into her beetle-black eyes. "There are others who think I've got the right idea – oh, yes. Just biding their time..."

The MLM exchanged looks of alarm; if what Hilda said was true, and there really *were* others out there who wanted to overturn the Monster Secrecy Act, then that was worrying indeed.

"And then we shall see who puts who in Reform school," the hag continued. "I'm thinking **Reform Level One:** *Good Monsters Who Don't Know (or Care) That They're Good* and **Reform Level Two:** *Good Monsters Who Need to Get in Touch with Their Bad Monster Instincts.* What do you think, Mummy?"

"I think you're mad," Mummy replied. "That'll *never* happen – we won't allow it!"

"We'll see," Hilda snarled menacingly, baring her blackened teeth. "Well, shall we get on with it, then?"

"Yes," Mummy agreed. "We've wasted enough time on your absurd ramblings. As I've said, you're not taking Theodora anywhere. I suggest you go at once – return to whatever hole you've been hiding in – and leave us alone. Otherwise I'll report you to the authorities."

"Oh," giggled the hag, "I don't think you will. For then I shall be forced to report *you*."

"Too late," said Mummy smugly. "Dracula's flying to Headquarters as we speak. We're reporting ourselves."

"You can't!" Theodora cried. "They'll send me away!"

"If I may," said Grimeny Cricket, clearing his throat. "Ever since that first letter arrived, we've been looking into past situations such as these – studying the old journals, the case law. We've found several instances in which exceptions have been made to the rules. We are nearly certain you will be allowed to stay."

"And we have a back-up plan if you're not," Marty added.

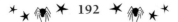

"No!" Hilda screeched, fury flushing her hollowed cheeks. At the sound of her scream, the skele-crow took flight, circling overhead. "Theodora is *mine*!" Hilda banged her walking stick on the ground three times.

And then, if you'll excuse my language, all hell broke loose.

What's that? You've never heard of hags having magical powers before? Well, then you've got a *lot* to learn about monsters.

It's not only witches who cast spells. It's true, however, that haggy powers are different from witchy powers. Hags can only use the elements (for those of you who sleep through your science lessons, the elements are earth, air, water and fire). And the element Hilda called upon now was earth.

As her walking stick struck the ground, the blades of grass beneath their feet began to twitch. Small stones and pebbles began to roll, followed by bigger rocks and chunks of gravel. The ground began to shake.

"E-earthquake!" Dexter choked out, shaking nearly as badly as the grass.

"I don't think so," said Sherman. "It's more likely to be a fissure."

Sherman was right, for as soon as he had spoken the ground split open between Hilda's feet, parting like the sea.

Before anyone could yell, "Get out of the way!" the crevice grew wider and wider, until it was large enough to fit a full-grown man.

Or a hobgoblin.

Remember the hobgoblins? They're about a metre tall

and nearly as wide, have skin as hard as armour and favour the double-edged axe as their weapon of choice. Small children are their favourite snack (and they have the flat, bone-crushing teeth to prove it). Theodora and Dexter were rather older than the hobgoblins preferred, but hobgoblins aren't all that picky.

Why am I talking about hobgoblins at a time like this? Because loads of them were streaming out of the crack in the ground, falling in line behind Hilda. And the earth wasn't just spitting out hobgoblins. Oh, no.

Spiders and centipedes and scorpions so large they made Sherman look like an ant came pouring out. The insects were followed by rats the size of raccoons and snakes as long as school buses. Did I mention there was also a skeleton slash zombie slash corpse army? Well there was, and as they climbed out of the fissure Theodora felt certain she and the MLM were done for. Yes, the good monsters of the MLM were

powerful,
and they looked
quite impressive
silhouetted beneath the
wings of the angel, but how
could the five of them possibly win against dozens
of evildoers?

"Theodora, Dexter – get behind us," Mummy
ordered, unsheathing two jewel-encrusted knives
Theodora recognized from the MLM's Ancient-
Curse-Breaking Room. The blades glinted
dangerously, though not nearly as dangerously
as the calculating expression masking Mummy's
usually pleasant features.

The children didn't need telling twice.

"Monsters – on my count. One," Mummy began,
as Grimeny Cricket raised
his scythe and Marty
extended his claws.

"Two," she continued,
Bandit baring his

fangs while Georgie
unhinged his jaw until
it was wide enough to hold a beach ball.

"Three."

They attacked. Marty reached the bad monsters
first, swiping his claws with deadly accuracy and

sinking his teeth into the neck of
any corpse foolish enough to
cross his path. Grimeny Cricket
hopped from snake to snake,
smiting them with his scythe.
Bandit was fearless, biting and
clawing the rats, while Georgie
swallowed the insects whole. And
Mummy – well, Mummy was amazing.
She hit and kicked and flipped over the hobgoblins,
slicing and dicing until their sickly orange
blood soaked the dirt.

"M-maybe we'll get out of this alive after all," Dexter whispered to Theodora.

But Hilda was not so easily beaten. She raised her walking stick into the air, waving it overhead as if she was trying to stir the clouds. There was a flash of lightning. The sky cracked open like an egg, pelting them with fat, heavy raindrops. The wind groaned, picking up speed and strength to form a funnel.

Yes, Hilda had called forth the element of air to create a tornado.

And it was heading straight for them.

Whirlwinds, Walls and Walking Sticks

"W-what should we do?" Dexter sobbed.

"I should think it obvious," said Sherman. "Run!"

"Watch the crack," Theodora called over her shoulder, dodging a hairy centipede and narrowly avoiding a hobgoblin as she tried to outstrip the tornado.

"Oh, no, you don't!" screamed the hag, whipping her cane through the air.

Over their laboured breathing the children heard the sound of something sizzling, like a drop of water hitting a smoking pan. The air in front of them seemed to shimmer.

"Ow!" they cried.

Hilda had erected an invisible wall, which Theodora and Dexter had run into face-first. They landed hard on the ground, the penknife flying from Dexter's hand. As if he'd been waiting for this to happen, the skele-crow dive-bombed the earth, grabbing the knife with his talons and cawing triumphantly.

"Your knife," Dexter moaned as the bird took to the skies.

"I've broken a monocle," sighed Sherman.

"We're having quite the party," Hilda cackled. "See what fun we could have?"

"You're mad!" Theodora cried over Hilda's manic laughter.

"N-now what?" asked Dexter, rubbing his bruised back.

"I don't know," said Theodora, wringing her hands and wishing the skele-crow hadn't taken their only weapon. "We're trapped! The tornado is getting closer and invisible walls are impossible to break through, unless you use magic or have—"

"The help of the Invisible Man?" asked a

disembodied voice. (I know, I know – there's another voice appearing as if from nowhere. But that's the whole point of having a battle in a graveyard – there are plenty of places to hide. Not that our newest arrival needed places to hide, but still!)

"Invisible Man, is that you?"

"At your service. I was swimming the English Channel when Owen found me and told me to come at once."

"C-can you help us?" begged Dexter, looking in entirely the wrong direction for their would-be saviour.

"And quick," Sherman added. "That tornado will be upon us any second." He nodded at the whirling, swirling funnel cutting a path towards them. It left a trail of destruction in its wake, scattering bones and headstone fragments everywhere (and the dust was making Dexter sneeze).

"I think that's a job for uuuuuus," sang Figaro, floating by with three phantoms and Pimms the Poltergeist.

"We'll help with the beasts," drooled Gabe,

arriving with several round-shouldered ghouls. "Ought to even the odds a bit."

"Count us in, mate," said Bob, the Head Gargoyle, leading the rest of the stone guardians into the fray.

"We'll catch that thieving skele-crow!" Sally added.

The ghouls and gargoyles ran into battle, and the ghosts gathered around the tornado. They clasped hands as if they were about to play a game of ring-a-ring-o'roses, sucking in great gulps of air as if trying to swallow it whole.

The Invisible Man began taking apart the invisible wall. (I have no idea how he did this; I can't see the Invisible Man any better than you can.)

"NO!" Hilda screamed so loudly it's a miracle her vocal cords didn't snap. She strode over to where the children kneeled, their clothing growing more sodden with each heartbeat. She towered over them, her terrible face contorted in rage. She raised her staff once more, delivering a final strike to the earth. Fire erupted from the top of her walking

stick, encircling Theodora, Dexter and Sherman in a ring of hungry, deadly flames.

They were well and truly trapped.

"Now," Hilda hissed, stalking towards them. "You will come with me, dearie. You shall put on your collar and walk with your lead and sleep in your cage. And if you're a good girl, perhaps I'll let you play with the other pets…"

Now, a lot of people, in finding themselves in this situation – you know, monster battle raging, tornado whirling, fire blazing, cornered by an evil hag – would have panicked. Not Theodora.

If anything, her resolve was strengthened. She jumped to her feet, her hair growing wilder by the second in the heat of the flames. She looked truly fierce. "I'll never go with you!" she yelled.

"Then you shall die along with your monsters," Hilda promised.

"You'll have to catch me first!" Theodora spun around, having decided what she was going to do only moments before. Bravely, and perhaps foolishly (it's a fine line, after all), she took a running leap through the flames, landing in a roll on the other side.

"And catch you I shall!" screeched the hag. For someone who was at least a dozen centuries old, Hilda moved with surprising speed, missing Theodora only by centimetres as they zigzagged between the tombs.

Theodora ran as if her life depended on it – which, I suppose, it did. But she soon realized she couldn't keep up the pace; despite her *very* advanced age, Hilda wasn't showing any signs of slowing, and Theodora was already out of breath, a painful stitch forming in her side. To an outsider looking in, the situation must have appeared hopeless. But, as you already know, Theodora is a very determined person and she, too, had more than one trick up her sleeve.

"Where are you going?" Mummy yelled, cutting off the head of a particularly ugly hobgoblin as Theodora raced by, Hilda hot on her heels.

"I've got a plan!"

"She's got a plan, Mummy," cackled the hag.

Steering clear of the worst of the battle, Theodora looped around the headstones, weaving a seemingly directionless path between them. But if you were paying attention, you would have noticed that she was carefully – ever so carefully – leading Hilda towards Georgie's plot. And although she was so tired her legs felt as if they would fall off, and she could barely get enough air into her lungs, Theodora put on a final burst of speed. Just before she reached the headstone, she came to an abrupt stop. She glanced down. The grave was empty.

Just as she'd hoped.

The hag didn't slow, her wicked laughter ringing across the cemetery. She made a final grab for Theodora, fingernails slashing through the rain.

But Theodora was ready for her. At the very last second, when it seemed Hilda had finally won, Theodora stepped sideways, just out of reach. The hag teetered on the edge of the grave, arms waving like helicopter propellers as she struggled to regain her balance.

And then Hilda fell down, down, down, into the grave.

Breathing hard, Theodora peered cautiously over the edge. Hilda was crumpled in a muddy heap some two metres below.

"My walking stick," moaned the hag, holding the broken pieces in her claw-like hands. "You'll pay for this!"

"I don't think so," Mummy huffed, joining Theodora at the edge of the grave. "In case you haven't noticed, your spells are broken. You're finished, Hilda."

Theodora looked around. It was true. The skeleton slash zombie slash corpse army was collapsing where it stood, turning to dust. The few hobgoblins who'd survived Mummy's attack were running back towards the fissure, hurtling themselves back inside while the giant insects, rats and snakes were crawling, scurrying and slithering after them. Within moments the crack had sealed, the seams of the earth merging together as if the break had never existed. The tornado stilled. The fire died. The invisible wall was gone.

The MLM had won; Hilda was defeated.

Now, in most books this would be the end of the story. But this isn't most books.

The Unravelling of the Plot

The rest of the MLM gathered around the stranded Hilda, Sally clutching the squawking skele-crow in her stone fist.

They all looked a little worse for wear. Sherman, of course, had cracked a monocle and lost his hat, though Dexter assured him these could be replaced. Grimeny Cricket had torn his cloak and Mummy's bandages were stained and beginning to unravel. Marty had broken several nails, Georgie looked more decrepit than ever and Bandit was covered in rat intestines. I have no idea as to the state of the Invisible Man, but I assume he was fine, if a little raw-fingered from tearing down the invisible wall.

"What happened to her corpse army?" asked Dexter, cleaning his glasses on the bottom of his

shirt (which was so filthy that all he succeeded in doing was dirtying the lenses even more). "Why did they turn to dust?"

"From dust they came, and to dust they returned," replied Grimeny Cricket. Seeing that Dexter was still confused, the bug added, "Hilda used her magic to tear those poor souls from their eternal sleep, forcing their bones to reform, their flesh to reattach, their bodies to reanimate… When her staff broke, so did her spell, and the undead returned to their slumber, at peace once more."

Dexter's brow was still furrowed, but again, that may just have been because he could barely see out of his glasses, which were nearly opaque with dirt. Before he could ask Grimeny Cricket to explain further, Figaro nodded at Hilda, singing, "What should we do with heeeeeer?"

"Let me take a bite out of her," Marty growled.

"Stay away from me, dog," Hilda screeched from the bottom of the grave.

"We'll take her back to the mansion and hand her over to Headquarters," said Mummy, glaring at the hag. "Let them deal with her."

"Nooooo," moaned Hilda. "You can't do that!"

"How do we get her out of there?" asked one of the ghouls.

As they pondered how to extract her, the sky returned to its usual blue. The clouds faded to mist, burning off entirely as the sun broke through.

"Someone will have to guard her. The rest can return to the mansion for tools," Mummy decided. "We can throw her a rope and pull her out, but we'll need handcuffs or something to bind her wrists."

"So little faith, Mummy?" the hag tittered madly.

"I have just one question," said Grimeny Cricket, turning to Hilda. "Where did you get the earwax?"

"I was wondering about that myself," said Theodora.

"The trolls, obviously. Had to throw you off my scent, didn't I? Classic misdirection," she said smugly. "Besides, it was easy. I just offered them each a pound of snot – their own noses get so very dry – and they were more than willing to make the trade. They sent it by post."

"Ewww," said Dexter and Sherman, thoroughly disgusted.

"How did you get the last letter to my school?" Theodora asked, remembering how the note had appeared just after the caretaker walked past as she and Dexter hid in the storage cupboard.

"The bird, of course," said Hilda, pointing at the skele-crow. "I had him spying on you in the form of a crow. He dropped the note through a window so it would look as if it had fallen from the caretaker's pocket. One of my more brilliant ideas," the hag giggled.

But a second later her shrieks of laughter turned to screams of fear. Two long-fingered, greyish-brown hands were clawing their way through the dirt, poking grotesquely through the soil like demented daisies. Hilda leapt to her feet, but the hands caught her round the ankles, jerking her back to the ground.

The hag grabbed a piece of her shattered cane, furiously bashing the hobgoblin's hands over and over. It was no use; the creature's grip would not weaken.

"Should we help her?" Theodora asked in horror. But a hobgoblin was already dragging Hilda beneath the surface, until only the whites of her eyes were showing.

Then the hag was gone, swallowed up by the earth she'd once commanded. Only the splintered ends of her walking stick remained, as powerless and insignificant as a child's wooden sword.

"Well, I guess we don't have to worry about getting her out any more," Marty said after a moment.

"Is she d-dead?" asked Dexter.

"Who knows?" Mummy replied. "Though I don't see how she could have survived. Hobgoblins are *very* dangerous…"

"But, then, so is Hilda," murmured Grimeny

Cricket, who wasn't so sure they'd seen the last of the wicked hag.

"Marty, Mummy – come quick!"

It was Wilhelmina, glamoured as a librarian and running at them full pelt.

"Wilhelmina, we've just finished," said Mummy. "You'll never guess who was behind—"

"Never mind that now!" Wilhelmina cried. "She's coming! Drink these, right away!"

"Who's coming?" drooled Gabe the ghoul.

"That old hag," said Wilhelmina, passing out small, smoking vials of potion to each of the monsters.

"B-but she's down there," said Dexter, pointing at the grave. "Or, at least, she was."

"Not her – the one from Theodora's school!"

Theodora and Dexter looked at each other in confusion. And then it clicked.

"Ms Frumple!" Theodora gasped. (You hadn't forgotten about her, had you?)

"W-what's she doing h-here?" stammered Dexter.

"I don't know, but it can't be good," Theodora

replied. "Ghosts and gargoyles – you've got to get out of here!"

"Riiiiiight you are," sang Figaro.

"We'll see you back at the house, mates," said Bob, taking to the skies with his fellow gargoyles (including Sally, still holding the skele-crow).

"Sherman, back in my bag – quick."

As Sherman crawled into the rucksack (keeping a safe distance from the torch) the rest of the monsters chugged their potions, gasping and shuddering as they transformed. It wasn't a moment too soon, for the iron gates were groaning open; Ms Frumple had arrived.

"Everyone, move out," Mummy ordered. "The last thing we need is a human discovering us standing around a hobgoblin-infested grave."

"Bandit, can you do me a favour?" asked Grimeny Cricket urgently.

"Meow."

"Thank you. If you could deliver these to the school," he said, handing Bandit two handwritten notes, one on plain stationery, the other on a colourful notecard. "Georgie, perhaps you should go too…"

"Eurg."

Georgie and Bandit sank into the shadows, slinking behind the tombstones as they made their way out of the graveyard and along the back roads to Appleton Primary. The rest of the glamoured monsters fell into formation, moving as one to meet Ms Frumple.

The head teacher was standing just inside the gates, staring at the ruins of the graveyard in stunned disbelief. "What on earth happened here?"

"Break-in," said Wilhelmina calmly. "We think it was kids – we saw some sweet wrappers and what not. The police should be here any minute."

Out of the corner of her eye, Theodora saw Marty pull a silver mobile phone out of his pocket. Falling back so he was slightly hidden from Ms Frumple's line of sight, the werewolf glamoured as a car salesman deftly dialled, murmuring softly into the phone. A few moments later, he slipped it back into his pocket, unnoticed by anyone except Theodora.

"Kids," repeated Ms Frumple softly. "Kids,

perhaps, who have sneaked out of school without permission? Kids, perhaps, who have repeatedly shown a flagrant disregard for the rules? Kids, perhaps, who are standing beside you?"

"Are you suggesting that Theodora and Dexter had something to do with this?" asked Mummy indignantly.

"Yes, I am," said Ms Frumple. "Are you aware of how many rules Theodora breaks?"

"I only break them when I have to!" Theodora protested.

"All children break rules occasionally," said Mummy stiffly.

"Of course," said Ms Frumple, nodding indulgently. "But not so often – nor so egregiously – as Theodora. In fact, this latest episode is so severe I think I shall have to recommend expulsion."

"You can't do that!"

"Outrageous!"

"And perhaps," Ms Frumple continued over their protests, "we should expel her friend as well." Her cold gaze slid to a horrified Dexter.

"That's not fair!" Theodora cried. "Dexter never does anything wrong!"

"Tut tut, such a big temper for such a little girl."

"I'm not a little girl!" Theodora yelled, stamping her foot.

"And a liar," Ms Frumple finished nastily. "Mr Adebola has obviously broken several rules, as he is here with you instead of in the classrom, where he belongs."

"Who says he belongs in the classroom?" growled Marty.

"It is now –" Ms Frumple paused, glancing down at her watch – "three o'clock in the afternoon on a school day. Neither Dexter nor Theodora has permission to be out of lessons today – I checked with the school secretary. As soon as Mrs Dullson realized two of her students were missing, she came straight to my office. Luckily several Year Six students saw Theodora leaving the school grounds and walking up the lane. As there's nothing up there besides the graveyard, she was easy to trace."

"Well, you'd better check again," said Mummy, her chin jutting forward as Theodora's did when she was angry. "Both Theodora and Dexter had permission to leave class at two o'clock today to accompany our family on a little outing."

"Oh?" challenged Ms Frumple, raising her eyebrows in disbelief. "And what 'outing' was that? I've never heard of a family 'outing' to a cemetery before…"

"I imagine the things you haven't heard of would fill a book, lady," snarled Marty.

"Now, now," Wilhelmina intervened, before things could take a turn for the worse. "No need for that, old boy. We take an annual outing to the Appleton cemetery," she said, directing her speech at Ms Frumple. "Generations of our family are buried here. Theodora's mum and I like her to have a sense of family history."

"I didn't realize you were related," said Ms

Frumple, smiling her crocodile smile. "Theodora's mother has an Egyptian accent."

"We're step-sisters," said Wilhelmina swiftly.

"I see. And why was Dexter with you?"

"Mrs Adebola thought it would be good for Dexter to see a graveyard up close," Mummy explained. "To help him get over his fear of them."

Dexter nodded mutely, avoiding Ms Frumple's narrowed gaze.

"Well, shall we head back to school and double check with the secretary?"

"Of course," Mummy agreed.

"And when we find that you have been less than honest – *then* we shall talk punishment. I believe Mrs Adebola will be arriving shortly." Ms Frumple marched across the litter-strewn grass, waiting by the gates for the rest to file out.

They were a glum and quiet group on the way back to the school.

"Secretary," said Ms Frumple, rapping sharply on the reception desk some fifteen minutes later.

"Yes, ma'am?" replied the secretary, her bleached-blonde hair piled high on her head in the shape of a beehive. "Did you need something else?"

"Yes," said Ms Frumple. "I'd like you to double-check the permissions list for today's absences. Specifically for Theodora Hendrix and Dexter Adebola."

"Hendrix," the secretary mumbled, snapping her gum beneath Ms Frumple's furious gaze. "And Adebola. Yup, I've got them right here."

"Excuse me? What did you say?"

"I've got them right here," repeated the secretary. "Hendrix and Adebola, both absent from two o'clock today."

"Impossible," snapped Ms Frumple. "Let me see those at once!"

"Here you are," replied the secretary, pushing two slips of paper at Ms Frumple with a shrug.

You might be interested to learn that one piece of paper was plain, and the other was a colourful notecard. Yes, thanks to Grimeny Cricket's quick thinking, and Bandit and Georgie's quick travels, two permission notes had slipped unnoticed into the

secretary's files (she'd been busy grabbing another stick of chewing gum from her bag, oblivious to the fanged cat slinking in through the window, landing soundlessly on her desk and depositing the papers before sneaking back out).

"But just an hour ago you said there weren't any!" Ms Frumple spluttered.

"I must have missed them. It was hectic, what with that child setting off the fire alarm and everything. I even missed my coffee break."

Ms Frumple glared at the woman, as if this wasn't the appropriate time to mention coffee breaks, missed or otherwise.

At that moment Mrs Adebola came sweeping into the room. She was dressed smartly in a tailored grey suit, her gele wrapped elegantly around her head. Ms Frumple's gaze flew to the scarf, staring at it as if it was something dangerous.

Mrs Adebola's eyes narrowed. "Yes?" she demanded. "Why have you asked me to come in? I'm missing a very important meeting."

"Then we shall not take up your time," said

Ms Frumple, her pale gaze lingering on Mrs Adebola's head.

"Mrs Adebola, did Dexter have permission to leave school today at two p.m. with the Hendrix family?"

Mrs Adebola was clearly confused. "Did Dexter have permission to – what are you talking about?"

"I see," breathed Ms Frumple, taking in the glamoured monsters' guilty faces. "Are you aware that your son left school today, followed Theodora  Hendrix – a known rule breaker – out of the school grounds, and caused a great deal of destruction to a local landmark?"

"Dexter did what…?" cried Mrs Adebola. She trailed off, eyes glazing over.

At the same time, Theodora heard Wilhelmina

whisper something that sounded suspiciously like, "*Hinkle-pinkle, fritzle-due.*"

Yes, Wilhelmina had cast a spell upon Mrs Adebola.

"Of course Dexter was with the Hendrix family," she said dreamily. "I wrote him a note." She shook her head, as if trying to clear it. "And Dexter would never destroy someone's property, landmark or otherwise," she snapped, sounding more like herself as the effects of Wilhelmina's spell faded. "Dexter, let's go. Theodora, we'll see you on Friday."

"Bye!" Theodora waved, grinning.

"Bye," said Dexter. "This was the best day of my life," he added in a whisper. "Tell Sherman I'll see him soon."

"Well," said Wilhelmina after the Adebolas' departure. "I guess that clears that up, doesn't it?"

"No, it doesn't," Ms Frumple fumed. "Something *funny* is going on here and I intend to find out what."

"She probably just forgot," Mummy shrugged. "Mrs Adebola has a very big job, you know."

"You did something," Ms Frumple hissed, banging a fist on the desk and ignoring the secretary's look of shock at her behaviour. "I know you did."

"Prove it," growled Marty.

"I can't," said Ms Frumple. "Not yet. But believe me, I will. And then I shall have this *monstrosity* of a child expelled," she said, scowling at Theodora, whom she seemed to find more offensive than the secretary's chewing gum and Mrs Adebola's gele put together.

"Ms Frumple," Mummy said warningly. "I would hate to have to report you to the school board for unprofessional conduct… Let's go, Theodora."

"Gladly."

They were nearly at the door when Ms Frumple called, "Ms Hendrix?"

Theodora turned back to the head teacher. "Yes?"

"I'll be watching you. If you put so much as a toe out of line…"

Theodora opened her mouth to reply, but decided there was really nothing to say to this – at least, nothing that Mummy wouldn't consider terribly rude. Instead, she gave a one-shouldered shrug and carried on through the door. As they left the office, she slipped her hand into Mummy's and asked, "Can we have pizza for dinner?"

"I think so," Mummy smiled.

You will be pleased, I am sure, to learn that there is only one more part to this story: the small matter of Dracula self-reporting the MLM in Transylvania, and Headquarters' decision regarding Theodora's and the monsters' fates.

You hadn't forgotten about that too, had you?

The Nose Knows

There was a lot going on, so I'll forgive you for overlooking the teeny, tiny fact that Dracula had flown to Transylvania for the express purpose of turning himself – and the rest of the MLM – in to Headquarters. He hadn't wanted to, of course. But when push came to shove, the monsters had agreed it was the only thing to do.

Mummy had said it best: "If the choice is between protecting ourselves or protecting Theodora, then we really don't have a choice at all."

"Hear, hear," agreed Sir Pumpkin-de-Patch. "We can't lose our Theodora."

"More like, we cannot allow Theodora to take matters into her own hands – as she has been known to do," clarified Grimeny Cricket. "It's our

fault she's in this mess in the first place. If only we had returned her to the humans as we'd planned…"

"If we'd done that, our lives would be very empty indeed," said Wilhelmina.

"Besides," said Mummy, "of all the places to abandon a baby, why choose a graveyard? It's almost as if whoever left her *meant* for her to be ours."

"Then we've made our decision," said Dracula, the shadows under his eyes deepening to the colour of an over-ripe plum. "I'll fly to Headquarters and finish this once and for all. Grimeny Cricket, if you could organize your research for me? I'll need to make a strong argument."

"Of course."

"And, Marty, be ready to go with Plan B, just in case."

"Understood," Marty grunted.

And so, several hours before the battle at the Appleton graveyard, Dracula had flown to Transylvania with a briefcase full of legal documents and a heart heavy with worry. But now he had

returned, and was waiting to share what had happened at Headquarters.

"There you are," he cried in relief, as the glamoured monsters climbed out of Mummy's sports car. "I went to the graveyard – a disaster zone! – and I went to the school, but they said you'd left half an hour ago, and then I came here and you weren't home … and … what *is* that smell?" He sniffed. "You've been around someone with very sour blood," he said, his nostrils flaring at the scent of it.

Mummy, Marty and Theodora each tried to answer Dracula's questions at the same time:

"It was Hilda," said Mummy. "*She* was the letter writer. She called forth a terrible monster army that destroyed the cemetery…"

"It's probably that foul Frumple woman's blood that you're smelling," said Marty. "Talk about sour…"

"We stopped for pizza," Theodora supplied, showing him the steaming cardboard boxes in her arms.

"But of course," said Dracula. "Er, perhaps we should move inside. I have some news."

The colour drained from Theodora's face, her skin turning the same chalk-white as the vampire. "Did Headquarters make their decision?" she asked, her teeth beginning to chatter despite the warm weather.

"They did," Dracula said gravely, leading the way into the mansion.

Mummy gave Theodora's shoulder a squeeze.

They gathered inside the Beelzebub Parlour where Helter-Skelter had lit a fire, warm and welcoming and so very different from Hilda's angry flames. Theodora placed the pizza boxes on the coffee table but made no move to open them (a first). Though she was filthy and guaranteed a stern talking-to from Helter-Skelter, she perched upon the edge of the sofa, giving Dracula her full attention. Sherman climbed out of her bag and onto her lap, pincers clicking together nervously.

"Well?" Mummy prompted.

Before Dracula could respond, Sir Pumpkin-de-Patch burst into the room.

The first thing Theodora noticed was that a

walnut-sized chunk of his head was missing.

The second thing she noticed was that he wasn't alone. Wrapped in his vine-y fingers was a hand the size of a dustbin lid, attached to an arm as thick as a tree trunk, attached to a boulder-shaped body, attached to an ugly head with two stunning eyes of sapphire (no, really – *actual* sapphires) and a shock of electric-blue hair.

Have you guessed what Sir Pumpkin-de-Patch was holding?

"A troll!" he cried, pulling the giant deeper into the room. "I found a troll!"

"What's this?" asked Dracula.

"I caught him prowling around the garden," said Sir Pumpkin-de-Patch.

"You're *supposed* to be watching the cubs," Marty retorted.

"The cubs are just fine. They're more than capable of taking care of themselves, I assure you," said Sir Pumpkin-de-Patch icily, pointing to the missing portion of his head.

"But why did you go into the garden in the first place? The Headless Horseman was making his rounds…"

Sir Pumpkin-de-Patch straightened. "I sent him away. His horse was trampling my prize-winning pumpkins! As Monster-Gardener-in-Chief, it's well within my rights to banish anything threatening the health of my plants. So I told him to get out and stay out."

The monsters rolled their eyes but held their tongues (it's a well-known fact that Sir Pumpkin-de-Patch's devotion to his plants – while admirable – borders on obsession).

"But how did you *catch* him?" asked Mummy, taking in the troll's enormous size.

"Lured him with dried basil," he replied, raising a wad of faded greens in his other hand. "I know Headquarters said all European Troll Cluster members are supposed to be under house arrest, but I couldn't shake the feeling that they were somehow involved."

"They *are* under house arrest," interjected the Invisible Man. "When I left the Highlands all four hundred members were locked inside Trollopolis Castle."

"Obviously not."

"Pumpkinhead's right," said Marty grudgingly. "*This* troll definitely isn't locked up."

"But *four hundred* trolls are," huffed the Invisible Man. "Which means we've got an even bigger problem."

"Yes," Dracula agreed. "As it appears there's at least one rambling about without Headquarters' knowledge."

"Two," corrected Helter-Skelter, entering the room with a troll identical to the first, except that it had emerald eyes and green hair. "He was in the pantry eating honey."

"Trolls," said Dracula, turning towards the

towering creatures. "You have trespassed on MLM property. Therefore you will answer our questions – truthfully. If you refuse, or if you're dishonest, we'll lock you in the dungeons and turn you over to Headquarters." ("We have *dungeons*?" Theodora whispered to an equally stunned Sherman.) "Do you understand?" Dracula asked, surveying the trolls with his fathomless eyes.

The trolls seemed to shrink under the vampire's gaze, docilely bobbing their heads.

"Why are you here?"

"A hag sent us."

The monsters exchanged knowing looks.

"Did this hag happen to be named Hilda?" asked Grimeny Cricket.

"How did you know?"

"We're asking the questions here. What is it you were supposed to do?"

"She gave us a lot of snot – valuable stuff, hag's snot – and all we had to do was send our earwax and walk around the MLM mansion today and the school across the way a couple times."

So Theodora and the MLM hadn't been wrong after all – a troll *was* involved. Two, actually.

"Very well," said Grimeny Cricket. "If there are no further questions, let us vote. All who agree the trolls have been truthful, and neither committed nor intended to commit any act so harmful as to warrant imprisonment, say 'I'."

"I," chorused the monsters.

"That's a majority. Trolls, you're free to go, though Headquarters will be informed of this."

"Or you could stay here," Mummy suggested.

Mutters of dissent rippled around the room.

Mummy turned to face the League. "It would be a good opportunity to learn more about how and why there are undocumented monsters roaming around," she said shrewdly. "Especially in light of what Hilda told us…"

"That's true," the monsters agreed. "That's a good point."

"However," said Mummy, suddenly stern as she shifted her attention back to the trolls. "As you have assisted a known MLM defector you'll be required to attend reform school if you accept."

"We'll think about it."

"Wonderful," said Mummy. "But, Dracula, now that *that* has been resolved – can you *please* tell us what Headquarters had to say about Theodora?"

Dracula hesitated, refusing to meet his family's eyes. He pulled something from his cape. It was a scroll, made from the same faded parchment as

that of the MLM Charter. He unrolled it slowly, and began to read.

The Verdict

To the members of the Monstrous League of Monsters.
It has been brought to our attention by one **Dracula
– Vampire**, hereafter called The Accuser, that the
members of the MLM including but not limited to:

Grimeny Cricket – Buggy Bringer of Death
Sir Pumpkin-de-Patch the Fourth – Pumpkinator
Marty – Werewolf
Figaro – Operatic Ghost
Pimms – Poltergeist
Wilhelmina – Witch
Helter-Skelter– Skeleton
Hamlet – Skull
Mousetrap – Raven
Gabe – Ghoul
Bob – Gargoyle

Sally – Gargoyle

Sherman – Tarantula

Georgie – Zombie

Bandit – Vampire Cat

Dracula – Vampire

Mummy – Mummy

... hereby known as The Accused, have knowingly, purposefully and unashamedly broken MLM Headquarters' **Rule Number One:** Keep monsters hidden from humans. *As per MLM protocol, a trial will be held. If found guilty by the MLM Justice Committee, hereafter known as The Committee, The Accused shall be remitted to the prisons of Transylvania for ever, unless The Committee sees fit to recommend a different sentence.*

"They can't do that!" Theodora cried, her eyes rounding in horror.

"There's more," said Dracula grimly.

"*The human in question, one* **Theodora Hendrix**, *hereafter known as The Human, shall be returned to her own race.*"

"No!" Theodora shrieked. "They can't send me away, we're a family!"

"Dracula, what are we going to do?" asked Mummy.

"Plan B it is," growled Marty, rising to his feet.

"I haven't finished," said Dracula shortly.

"*However, The Accuser has also brought to our attention the fact that there were extenuating circumstances leading The Accused to disregard* **Rule Number One** *in favour of* **Rule Number Two:** *Protect humans from bad monsters. Furthermore, The Accused took additional steps to make suitable arrangements for the Human – including seeking her relatives and assessing their human neighbours (deemed unfit due to excessive cleanliness, vegetable eating and news watching) – before electing to keep her.*"

"You did?" asked Theodora in surprise. "You tried to find my birth parents?"

"Yes," said Mummy distractedly. "We put an advert in the paper and hired a private detective, but nothing ever came of it."

"If I may," Dracula huffed, glaring at the lot of them.

"*Taking this information into account, Headquarters has made an executive decision: The Human may remain at the MLM mansion, and The Accused are hereby cleared of any and all wrongdoing. However, Headquarters will be conducting an investigation on site at the MLM mansion to ensure there is no pattern of rule breaking. A Committee investigator will be arriving shortly.*"

Having finally reached the end, Dracula released the bottom of the scroll, the paper rolling up like a yo-yo.

"So what does this mean?" asked Theodora, who was struggling to understand all of the terminology in the note (to be fair, I'm not sure I understood all of it myself – and I have extensive training in these things).

"It means," said Grimeny Cricket gently, "that you can stay. And that we won't be thrown into prison," he added over the monsters' cheers.

A smile split Theodora's dirt-streaked face. Suddenly ravenous, she scooted forward on the sofa, propping open the pizza boxes. She was reaching

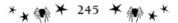

for the biggest – no, cheesiest – no, pepperoniest – slice when Marty snatched it out from under her hands, grinning. "Hey," she said in mock annoyance. "That was mine!"

"You snooze, you lose," Marty sniggered, taking a bite.

"I never snooze," Theodora giggled, reaching for another piece.

"I do," said Sherman. "Especially on school days."

"I think a party is in order," said Mummy.

Theodora and Sherman cheered.

"You're still grounded," Mummy told her. "Keeping secrets from us – especially big, dangerous secrets – is never OK."

Theodora's face fell.

"However, I think it can wait until tomorrow. Tonight, we're going to celebrate being together again. Helter-Skelter?"

But Mummy needn't have bothered calling – the butler was already there, arms overflowing with dozens of black balloons, orange streamers and purple crackers.

"I'll haaaandle the muuuuuusic," sang Figaro, already floating towards the music chamber to gather the other ghosts.

"Meow meow meow," said Bandit, which probably meant, "Georgie and I will get some candy-floss for dessert."

"I'll get the cubs," said Marty. "They love a good party."

"You keep those little *monsters* away from me," cried Sir Pumpkin-de-Patch.

And that, my friends, is the end of our story.

Almost.

E.S.M.A

An Offer You Can't Refuse

And so life returned to normal – well, as normal as it can be in a house full of monsters. True, Ms Frumple was still sniffing around. And, yes, Headquarters would be arriving soon to conduct their investigation. But on the bright side, the torat cards were behaving normally again; the crow and the cloaked figure (which we now know was a hag) had vanished.

You're wondering what happened to Hilda?

I'm sorry to say I don't know. It looked like she was gone for good, but rumour has it she escaped. A hobgoblin with a sizable lump on his head was found beside Georgie's grave, and the pieces of her cane were gone by the time the Monster Activity and Detection Crew arrived (I'll have to tell you about them some other time – I have already detained you

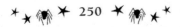

long enough). I'm told Headquarters has sent the Headless Horseman on a reconnaissance mission to find her, or to at least find the hobgoblin that supposedly ate her... We may never know what really happened.

OK, so maybe everything wasn't *entirely* back to normal. But as Sir Pumpkin-de-Patch said, they would deal with things when they had to, and they would deal with them together, as they always did.

So now you know the truth, the whole truth – not the watered-down version your parents have been telling you. And the truth is that there are monsters among us. They come in all shapes and sizes. Sometimes they even come in the form of people (ahem, Ms Frumple).

I know you're wondering why I've told you all of this.

Allow me to introduce myself. My name is Agent Charles Holmes, and I run the Eye Spy Monster Agency (yes, it was my business card Theodora stumbled upon in Dracula's office).

The agency is busier than ever. There's been more

monster activity recently than we've seen in years –
decades, even – and not just between humans and
monsters, but between the monsters themselves.
And there's more, much more, but I can't tell you
about it just yet.

Stop badgering me! I said I can't talk about it.
Honestly, I *could* – but then I'd have to kill you.
That is … unless…

Do you want to join us? The Eye Spy Monster
Agency, I mean. I really think you've got what it
takes, and frankly we could use the help. Give it a
try – what's the worst that can happen?

Fine, you might get chased by zombies. And,
yes, a hag might try to keep you as a pet. And, OK,
you might have to stare down a vampire. But it
will be an exciting – no, terrific – no, stupendous –
opportunity. It'll be worth your while, I promise.

Just do me one small favour:

Don't tell your parents I've made you this offer.
They won't be pleased. Not at all. They'll say it's
too dangerous. They'll say you're too young. But
Theodora Hendrix is proof that age doesn't matter

– not when you've got guts and brains and friends that have your back.

So, do we have a deal?

ACKNOWLEDGEMENTS

First and foremost, thanks to my amazing – no, fabulous –
no, *extraordinary* – agent and friend, Alice Sutherland-Hawes,
for believing in me and Theodora. You're a total rock star.

Thanks to the entire team at Walker Books, especially my
fantastic editors, Emma Lidbury and Frances Taffinder.
I cannot even begin to describe how much I appreciate
your vision, enthusiasm and patience. To Chloé Tartinville
and Rebecca Oram for the incredible design and publicity.
To Chris Jevons, illustrator extraordinaire, for bringing
Theodora Hendrix to life in such a spooktacular manner.

To my early readers, Jessica B. Caldwell, Jessica Taylor,
Megan D'Antuono and my lovely friends – you know who
you are – for allowing me to babble on and on (and on)
about Theodora, thank you. To Sylwia Tyburska, without
whose support I would have far less time to write. To the late
Robert E. Sloat for teaching me to "just show up"; I did.

Thanks to my family, whose antics have provided enough
material for several lifetimes (ahem, Tappy Jordan), especially
my late, beloved grandfather, Russell Kopyscianski,
who never doubted that I would become an author,
and my mother, Tamara Kopy Chilelli, who read Every.
Single. Draft. And last but never least, to my wonderful,
exceedingly patient husband, Todd Coletto: your constant
encouragement, humour and love have meant the world to
me. I couldn't have done it without you.

Jordan Kopy is a born and raised New Yorker who resides in London with her husband and poorly behaved (but lovable) cat. A financial services professional by day, she spends her nights with ghouls, witches and the occasional evil hag. Jordan is currently writing the second book in the Theodora Hendrix series.

Chris Jevons loved drawing from an early age, inspired by Saturday morning cartoons and Disney animated features. After studying art, design and animation at university, Chris worked as a graphic designer and a 2D animator before pursuing a career in children's publishing. Chris illustrates picture books and fiction for a variety of publishers and lives and works in Harrogate.